Windsor Heights

Book 3

Moon and Midnight

This book was written for all children everywhere

who have faith—stubborn faith—

and for those who don't,

that they may find it.

— Lisa Long

Windsor Heights

Book 3

Moon and Midnight

Lisa Long

Illustrations by Marian Long

Windsor Heights Books

Windsor Heights Book 3– Moon and Midnight

By Lisa Long

Copyright © 2017 by Lisa Long

ISBN: 978-0-9753566-2-3

Published by:
Windsor Heights Books,
Riverside, CA
www.windsorheightsbooks.com

Illustrations by Marian Long

Author's Note:

This story depicts real persons and events. Permission to appear on these pages has been received from all named individuals.

Printed in the United States of America

WHAT OTHERS ARE SAYING

"Convincing details and believable dialogue!"

— Cricket Books

"Wonderful stories full of warmth and understanding!"

— Royal Literary Publications

"Miranda begs for just one more chapter but I already told her we are reading one chapter a night as a family. Luke listens and laughs and waits for an illustration. My husband even listens. I really think you are a gifted writer."

— Debbie Heise, mother of Miranda,10, and Luke,6

"Dairean has had trouble reading in the past but she won't put your books down. She reads them at night until she falls asleep. I really feel like you wrote those books specifically for her."

— Dana, mother of Dairean, 10

"I really love your books, they are my favorite. I wouldn't read any other books. I love the part at the end of Book One when you say, 'Windsor Heights, here we come.' I read them late at night and I don't want to put them down. I'm thinking of reading them again."

— Dairean, 10

"Samantha always asks for one more chapter when we are reading at bedtime. I loved the robbery chapter and the gun was hilarious. Samantha made me lock all the doors and windows that night after we read that chapter I really think they can be adult books as well as children's books."

— Judy, mother of Samantha, 6

"I loved Book One with all the detail and I stayed up until 11pm one night just to finish Book Two."

— Tina Peters, mother and grandmother

"I loved the part in Book Two where the mother had the gun. That was so funny."

— Kevin Hetrick, 9

"We read a chapter every night at bedtime. Calvin really relates to Beau catching lizards and he thinks Jeff is so funny. He laughs out loud and even cried in one chapter."

— Christen Grover, mother of Calvin, 5

"I really enjoyed Books 1 and 2 and look forward to Book 3. They brought back a lot of memories and I think they would be great in our school library."

— Principal of Calvary Church of Santa Ana

"Besides science fiction, Book 1 is my favorite book I ever read."

— Timmy Courtney, 11

"She couldn't put the book down. She stayed up late and read it in her bed until her eyes closed. She hid from her little sister and her friends to finish reading the book. She said that she felt like it was her life."

— Linda, grandmother of two young girls

Contents

ACKNOWLEDGEMENTS

I would like to thank God for inspiring me and for giving me more than I ever dreamed of. I would like to thank my children – Lindsay, Jeffrey and Beau – for without them, this book would not have been possible.

I would also like to thank my mom for graciously accepting the assignment of illustrator. As a child I would always ask her to draw for me—a horse, a flower, anything. This book would not be complete without her drawings.

Chapter 1

Moon and Midnight

Lindsay and Midnight seemed to fit together perfectly. Like the last two pieces of a puzzle, they completed each other. After all, she had prayed a long time to have a horse, and Midnight was a true answer to her prayers. Midnight was 19 years old when he was given to Lindsay. The black gelding was older and more used up than some would want, but to Lindsay he was everything she ever dreamed of.

"Hey, Lindsay," her mother, Lisa, called from the back of her horse Moon, "isn't it kind of cool that both of our horses' names start with the same letter and our names start with the same letter?"

"Slow down, Mom, I can barely hear you," hollered Lindsay, who was riding Midnight behind her.

Lindsay and Lisa were out on their very first trail ride together, heading west on the Gage Canal in the middle of a forest of orange groves in Windsor Heights. The big, orange-red sun was down deep in the purple, blue, and pink streaked sky. The tall palm trees scattered on distant hills looked like fireworks lining the horizon.

Moon didn't want to slow down or stop. After all, he was a racehorse. Lisa pulled on her reins, but still Moon jigged on ahead as if he was in a rush to get somewhere. "Excuse me, Moon, but I would like to stop for a minute." Lisa said in a polite, yet frustrated tone of voice as she pulled even harder on her reins. Moon stopped but he didn't stand still. He turned sideways, shuffled his feet and began bobbing his head up and down. Lindsay and Midnight plunked along at a steady pace and caught up.

"Now what did you say about our names?" asked Lindsay.

"I said, isn't it cool that our horses' names and our names both begin with the same letter?" repeated Lisa as she continued to fight off Moon's urge to not stand still.

"Oh yeah," replied Lindsay with a smile, "that is cool. Hey, we can call them M and M for short."

Lisa let Moon walk on down the trail, staying as close to Lindsay and Midnight as possible. "Mom, why are you holding your reins so tight?" Lindsay asked.

"Because," Lisa said gritting her teeth, "this horse doesn't seem to know how to walk. You want to see a loose rein?" Lisa dropped her reins and Moon immediately began trotting. "Whoa! Moon, walk!" demanded Lisa. As Lindsay laughed, Lisa stopped Moon and waited again for Lindsay to catch up. "I really don't think it's funny," Lisa said, "or fun for that matter. This horse has no idea how to walk or stop. All he wants to do is trot and run."

"Gosh Mom, Midnight will walk or stop when I ask him, and look how loose my reins are," Lindsay said as she proudly displayed the looseness of her reins.

"Well, I'm glad you're enjoying yourself," Lisa said with a fake smile on her face. "Obviously your horse is much nicer than mine. I feel like I have blisters forming under my gloves and he is killing my back from his jigging."

Even though Lisa was having a bit of difficulty with her horse, she didn't want the moment to be spoiled. Trying to ignore her horse's unwanted behavior, she did her best to make small talk. "Have you ever seen such incredible colors in a sunset?"

Lindsay gazed off into the distance and shook her head.

"Lindsay, do you know what direction we're going?"

"Um, straight?" Lindsay replied.

"We're going west."

"How can you tell?" wondered Lindsay.

"Because I always remember Grandma telling me that 'the sun rises in the east and sets in the west.' And we are heading straight at the setting sun."

Just as Lisa said that, Moon stopped dead in his tracks and didn't move a muscle. He pricked his long, brown ears straight up, listening to something in the orange grove. He flared his big nostrils in and out, trying to pick up a scent. Lisa sat still to let him see what ever it was he'd heard. Lindsay and Midnight stood still beside them. Just then, a grove worker walked out from behind an orange tree and startled Moon. In an instant, Moon sprung sideways, turned around and headed for home. "Whoa! Whoa!" Lisa yelled, pulling Moon to a stop. She turned him around and walked him reluctantly back to the same spot. Lindsay laughed again.

"Oh, Mom, that was so funny. Your arms were flapping like chicken wings and everything!"

Lisa put her hand over her heart, "That scared me half to death! I am glad this is entertaining to you, but it feels like I just lost a heart valve!"

Lindsay laughed again and then bent over Midnight's neck and gave him a big hug. "Mom, Midnight didn't get afraid, not one bit when that man walked out from behind the tree."

"Oh gee, Lindsay, you don't say," Lisa said sarcastically. Lindsay giggled some more and stroked Midnight's mane. "Walk, Moon!" demanded Lisa, trying to enjoy the scenery.

It was late summer and the orange trees were already set with hundreds of small green balls that would grow into big beautiful oranges by Christmas time. "I can't believe the orange trees here, Lindsay. This place is amazing, don't you think?" Lindsay nodded. "Seriously, have you ever seen so many rows of orange trees and palm trees?" Lisa continued before Lindsay could answer, "You know what my favorite thing about this place is though, Linds? The canal." Lisa walked Moon over to the edge of the canal so she could get a closer look.

"Mom, I wouldn't walk that close to the canal," Lindsay warned.

Moon's hoof knocked a small dirt clod off the edge of the dirt road, tumbling it into the water. Lisa continued walking unworried. "Look, Lindsay! Moon likes the canal. He keeps wanting to walk right on the edge."

Lisa looked at Lindsay and smiled, "I think I'll call him 'Cliff Hanger.'" Lindsay sighed, "Suit yourself," and continued walking Midnight at a safe distance from the canal's edge.

On the way home from their ride, Lisa and Lindsay talked about Lindsay's first horse, Fresno, and how she loved her but how she already knew that Midnight and her were meant for each other. Lisa talked about her old horse Indian and how he was the perfect horse. "When I get to heaven, Indian will be waiting for me at the gate. I really believe that, Lindsay. Haven't you heard that old saying that everyone will have a horse waiting for them at heaven's gate. So, mine will be Indian. What about you?"

"Well, that's a hard question because I loved Fresno, but Midnight is my very own horse. He'll be at heaven's gate. Only one thing though. He

won't be old, he will be like four years old or something," Lindsay said thoughtfully.

"Oh yeah, Indian will be four years old, too."

Moon and Midnight were walking side-by-side along the dirt road, with Lisa and Lindsay enjoying their conversation, when Moon suddenly stopped, frozen like a statue, except for his ears. He twitched one ear this way and one ear that way, as if they were radar antennas picking up a sound that no one else could hear. Lisa settled down into her saddle and fastened her hands tighter around her reins. "Keep Midnight right next to me," Lisa said cautiously. Lindsay strategically moved Midnight as close to Moon as possible. Lisa stroked the side of Moon's neck and tried to reassure him. "You're all right, there's nothing to be so concerned about."

"Can you hear that, Mom? Listen … it sounds like Anne."

As the voices drew closer, sure enough, it was Lindsay's trainer, Anne, her voice carrying right over the top of the orange trees. Moon still did not move a muscle; he waited until he could see who was talking … Anne and a friend out trail-riding.

"Well, hi, Lindsay, hi, Lisa!" Anne yelled in her familiar, unmistakable voice, "It's good to see both of you out riding! Hey, that saddle I gave you fits you, but I can see right now that Moon will need more of a pad than that flimsy thing you've got on him. Believe me, you don't want him to getting a sore back." Without hardly taking a breath, Anne went on, "And, Lindsay, you have Midnight looking fabulous!"

Lindsay smiled and stroked Midnight's mane, "I put show shine on his mane."

"Well, sweetheart, in all honesty, that's not the best stuff to use on your horse, I mean it's all right to use on his mane and tail, but don't put it on his back because your saddle will slip. Hey, if you're interested, there's a horse show coming up this spring that I'll be going to."

"Really?" Lindsay wondered enthusiastically.

"Yes, you and Midnight can do it too, but you'll need weekly lessons starting immediately to be prepared in time," replied Anne.

Lisa joined in, "Are you sure, Anne? I mean, Midnight can't even really jump."

"I know. That's why I said they need lessons *now*," said Anne dramatically emphasizing with hand movements. "And you know," Anne raised her eyebrows while looking at Lisa on Moon, "you could even do the show on Moon, but *you* would need lessons like twice a week," added Anne with a laugh while she picked up her reins. "I'll give you a call to set something up. Let's go, Centurion!" she said as she prompted her big gray horse to start walking. Anne and her friend continued down the trail, gabbing all the way.

Lindsay looked at her Mom with raised eyebrows. Lisa smiled at Lindsay and chuckled, "It's unbelievable how her voice just travels through all these trees."

Lindsay laughed. "Mom, do you think we can really start lessons again?" she asked hopefully.

"I think that would probably be a good idea. Do you want to try a little canter here?"

"Okay," Lindsay said, "I go first."

Lindsay began trotting and then Midnight broke into a nice canter. Lisa asked Moon to canter just like Midnight but instead he fought for his head and tugged on his reins to catch up to Midnight. Lisa passed Lindsay, all the while trying to slow Moon down. Suddenly Moon shot his head straight down to the ground and began bucking. "Whoa! Whoa!" Lisa sat back and pulled Moon's head up and brought him to a stop. Again Lisa put her hand over her heart, "I think I just lost another heart valve."

Lindsay laughed. "When Midnight saw Moon start bucking, he gave me a buck, too. That was fun!"

"No, *that* was scary! Seriously, this is not the way I remember riding! If Dad likes this horse so much, then he can have him!" Lisa exclaimed. "Let's just walk the rest of the way home."

"When we get home, I'm going to give Midnight a bath." added Lindsay excitedly.

Bathing a horse isn't hard. Or at least it never had been before. Fresno used to enjoy her bath and Lindsay enjoyed bathing her. When Lisa and

Lindsay got home, Lindsay asked her Mom, "Where should I tie Midnight for his bath? There really isn't a good place to tie a horse, and there's no wash rack like I used with Fresno."

Lisa and Lindsay walked around with Midnight in his halter, looking for just the right spot to tie him, which seemed to be in front of their house on a low fence. Lindsay tied Midnight's lead rope to a rickety 2-by-4, which was meagerly nailed into equally rickety posts. Midnight looked suspicious as Lindsay turned on the hose. She began to spray Midnight with the chilly water and he began to snort, sounding more like a bull than a horse. Suddenly he pulled back with all his might and tore the piece of wood right off the posts. He stood scared, with the 2-by-4 dangling off the end of his lead rope.

"Lindsay! Back up, that wood has nails in it!" shouted Lisa as she ran to grab Midnight.

Lisa calmed Midnight down and took the 2-by-4 off his lead rope. "Here, you hold him and I'll spray him," Lisa suggested. Lindsay didn't say a word, and just stood holding the rope. Midnight

began to move around to avoid the hose, and twice nearly stepped on Lindsay's toes. "Lindsay, please hold him still."

"He won't!" exclaimed Lindsay.

Midnight swished his tail and stepped left and right. He held his head high and snorted. His eyes got big enough that the whites of his eyes showed.

"Lindsay, if you can't handle your horse on the ground, then you shouldn't even ride him!"

Lindsay tried to handle Midnight the best she could. She pulled on his lead rope and pleaded with him. Lisa became increasingly frustrated as both of them were now wetter and dirtier than the horse, "Look, Lindsay, if Midnight moves left, then you move right and push him back. He should not be allowed to do what he's doing!"

As Lindsay began to cry, Lisa said, "Sorry, Lindsay, but I don't feel sorry for you. You have to learn to be the boss of your horse or he'll walk all over you."

Finally, after the horrific bath experience was over, Lindsay and Midnight both began to calm down. The big orange sun was now half gone and slowly but surely disappearing. Midnight's soaking wet body began to shiver and tremble as he stood tied to a tree. He wrinkled up his nose and moved his mouth in a funny way while he dried.

Lindsay's face was all red and splotchy from crying, but she continued on her mission to have Midnight look just the way she wanted him to. She brushed his forelock, mane, and tail until every strand hung untangled; she trimmed the end of his tail with scissors so that it looked thick. Then she combed his jet black coat so that every hair went in the right direction. Lastly, she took a soft cloth and wiped Midnight's eyes and nostrils. Satisfied with her work, Lindsay gave Midnight a carrot.

Lindsay on the other hand was a disaster. Her hair and face were messed up, her clothes and boots were soaked through, but she didn't care. All she cared about in that moment was Midnight.

Chapter 2

Anne's Hill

Lindsay never wanted Anne to sell her house on Madison Street because she liked Anne's house and property. She liked seeing all of the horses and people who rode there everyday. But sometimes things just change even if no one wants them to. Anne now lived in a little house with just one acre on Grace Street, which was closer to the Wrights than Madison Street. This was good because they didn't have a horse trailer. If Lisa and Lindsay wanted a lesson, they could ride over to Anne's house.

On the day of their scheduled lesson, Lisa picked up the kids from school in her riding attire; tight stretchy pants and tall black boots.

"Mom, why are you wearing your riding boots?" Jeffrey asked with a grin, getting into the van.

"Because Lindsay and I have a lesson today right when we get home. By the way, Lindsay, we have our first lesson today at four. That means right when we get home, you'll need to hurry up and change. I'll get the horses ready. Okay?"

Lindsay's eyes got big and she took a deep breath, "All right."

As Lisa drove home slightly faster than usual, she talked to the kids and grilled them as usual with questions about their day at school. "So, Jeffrey, how are your walking skills going? Are you getting around faster without your crutches?"

"I guess," responded Jeffrey.

"I hope you're putting full weight on your leg like you're supposed to be doing."

"Mom, he's not," narked Lindsay. "I saw him limping at recess."

"Jeffrey, you broke your leg over four months ago, you need to start walking straight, concentrating on using both legs equally," reprimanded Lisa.

"I am," Jeffrey replied sheepishly.

"All right, Jeffrey, but if I have to go to school and watch you at recess to make sure you're walking right, I will," warned Lisa. "Aren't you glad that you don't have to use your crutches any more? I'm sure your armpits are happier." The kids chuckled. "Jeffrey, when we get home, I want you to keep an eye on Beau until Dad gets home, which shouldn't be too long, okay?"

"Okay," agreed Jeffrey, "but what if he doesn't listen?"

"He will," assured Lisa looking at Beau. "I already explained to him that he has to listen to you." Beau nodded.

By the time Lisa and Lindsay were on their horses, they had about 30 minutes to make it to their lesson. "Anne hates it when people are late to their lesson," Lindsay said as they walked their horses down the side of their property right next to the orange grove.

"Lindsay, I am fully aware of that," acknowledged Lisa. "Maybe we should trot when we get to a good spot."

"Okay," Lindsay said enthusiastically.

Moon still wanted to go faster than Lisa cared for, and seemed to be suspicious of everything along the way. Lisa did her best to keep up with Lindsay, who gracefully kept stride with Midnight posting in her saddle to the rhythm of her horse's trot. "Clickety clack, clickety clack," Moon and Midnight's hooves sounded. "Lindsay, how do I look? Am I doing it right?" shouted Lisa over the hoof beats.

Without ever breaking stride, Lindsay turned her head to watch her mother and began to laugh. "Keep your elbows from flapping, Mom."

Lisa was now breathing hard and beginning to lose her balance a little. "Lindsay, I think I need to stop. Seriously, I can't do it anymore."

Lindsay asked Midnight to slow down to a walk, and Lisa argued a bit with Moon until he began to walk, too. "Oh my goodness," sighed Lisa, pushing the visor of her helmet up out of her eyes. "This is way harder than I thought it would be."

Lindsay reached down and stroked Midnight on the side of his neck, "Good boy, Midnight." Midnight's eyes blinked and he licked his lips with his soft pink tongue.

"Gosh, Lindsay, Midnight is so sweet. Every time you pet him, he licks his lips." Lindsay petted Midnight again and watched to see if he would do it again.

"Good boy, Moon," Lisa said enthusiastically, patting her horse on the side of his neck.

"Good boy? Mom, he is *not* a good boy. Midnight is a good boy."

"I know, but maybe if I make him think he is, he will be," reasoned Lisa. "Oh, here's Grace Street. Now be careful and stay on the side of the street."

When Lisa and Lindsay arrived at Anne's house, they got off their horses. Anne had a very steep concrete driveway that led up to a big chain link fence. Mother and daughter walked their horses up to the fence and tried to swing the big fence open. Moon didn't like standing on the steep concrete driveway and began to fuss, which made

Lisa nervous. "Lindsay, back up! I can't open the gate with you and Midnight standing in the way."

"Well, I can't move with Moon standing there."

Lisa growled under her breath in frustration, "Here, you hold Moon while I open the gate," Lisa said, giving Lindsay Moon's reins.

But instead of accepting them, Lindsay held out Midnight's reins. "No, you hold Midnight and I'll open the gate."

The next obstacle was an entire driveway of big gray rocks. Both Moon and Midnight walked delicately through the rocks, especially Moon. He began to limp on the hard rocks, even stopping to see what was hurting his feet. Step-by-step, they walked to the back of Anne's property when Moon decided he didn't want to go any further. "Hi, guys! Come on back." called Anne.

"These rocks are hurting Moon's feet," Lisa yelled to Anne.

"Those rocks are fine, and they're not hurting his feet. I walk my horses over those rocks everyday and they're perfectly fine. Now get him moving and come on back!"

Lisa tugged on Moon's reins until he finally walked with her to Anne's arena, which was situated on top of a hill. Anne smiled at the sight of Lisa and Lindsay on their new horses at her new house. "This is going to work out great. How do you like the arena? I made it all by myself and I think it's just fabulous. I was going to get sand in here, but I decided that I liked the soil just the way it is. Not too hard and not too soft," Anne said, stomping her foot in the dirt displaying its texture. "I know, I know, it's not as big as the one at my other house, but frankly, this is all I need. As a matter of fact, if you can control your horse in a small arena, then you'll never have any problem in a large arena."

Uncertain, Lisa and Lindsay nodded. "Anne, do you still have jumps?" Lindsay asked.

Anne smiled a smile that she could hardly contain. "Do I have jumps? Sweetheart, of course I have jumps, and plenty of them." Anne motioned for Lisa and Lindsay to walk over to the far end of her arena. Lisa and Lindsay stood quietly looking over Anne's hill, and Lindsay's jaw dropped open at what she saw.

"They said I couldn't do it. They said that I would never be able to make this slope into a jump field, and they were wrong, I did it!" announced Anne proudly. "I know it looks scary now, but *believe me*," Anne said with every fiber in her being, "I have jumped every jump out there and once you accomplish this jump course, I can honestly guarantee you that you will never, *never* be afraid of anything else in your life!"

"I don't know Anne," sighed Lisa.

"What I want both of you to do right now, is to just walk around the outside of the jump field. Just to get used to it. All right? Go ahead, you'll be fine," assured Anne motioning them to begin walking.

Lisa and Lindsay walked their horses over the edge of Anne's hill and started down hill on a small path right against a 5-foot chain link fence. Lisa breathed a loud breath, exhaling her nervousness. "I can do this, yes, I can do this," she said, trying to convince herself.

"Is Anne nutso? If she thinks I'm going to jump Midnight over that," Lindsay said pointing to some big barrels lying awkwardly down on their side, "she's crazy!"

"This actually looks like a sinking ship," Lisa commented as she tried to console Moon, who was now sweating and walking sideways. "Lindsay, keep Midnight close to Moon. He's starting to get freaky."

Anne hollered from the top of her hill, "Okay, guys, come back up here and let's begin your lesson."

When they walked back to the top of hill, there were two more people there for the lesson. Moon was now bobbing his head up and down and stepping sideways. "Honey, can you get your horse to stand still?" Anne asked.

Lisa jerked on her reins and tried to keep Moon from bumping into anyone, "I'm trying, Anne, but he just seems to have a mind of his own."

"Oh," Anne said with a funny look on her face, "Well then, let's begin."

Lisa jumped off of Moon, "You know what, Anne, I'm just not up to this today. Can I put him in one of your empty corrals?"

"Sure, but he's not going to learn anything in there."

Lisa felt better being off of her horse, now she could concentrate on watching Lindsay. It had been a long time since the last time she had watched her daughter in a lesson.

"I want everyone to watch Carol do this course on Noah. He's twenty-five years old and they have done this course before," Anne announced. Lindsay looked at her mother as if to remind her that Noah was the horse she used to ride. Lisa nodded. Carol began cantering down hill on her little Arabian, "That's right, Carol. Now sit back, sit back, wait, wait, that's right," shouted Anne in her megaphone. "Now after the corner, take the barrels."

Carol maneuvered Noah around the tight turns and jumped the barrels, and then she proceeded to gallop up the hill to another awkward fence. "Yes, Carol, keep that pace and get ready, because he's going to take it … and … yes! That's it! Beautiful!" Anne was glowing. "Do you believe me *now* when I tell you this can be done? Lindsay dear, it's your turn."

Lindsay's eyes grew and she seemed to lose all the color in her face.

Lisa walked over to Anne, "Anne, Midnight doesn't know how to jump. You're not going to ask her to do what Carol just did, are you?"

"Oh no, not yet, Lindsay sweetie, bring Midnight over here," Anne asked.

As Lindsay walked Midnight over to Anne, she began to cry.

"Sweetie, look, you don't have to do that, but crying is not going to do anyone a bit of good. Now, does your horse like water?" Unable to speak, Lindsay shrugged her shoulders. Anne patted Lindsay's thigh and looked up at her blotchy face, "Did you see my water jump?" she asked delicately. Lindsay nodded. "Why don't we see if Midnight will walk through it, okay?" Anne led Midnight by the reins over to the water jump. "Now, all I want you to do, Lindsay, is just to walk through it and step up on the bank. You don't need to trot or canter. He can do this at a walk," assured Anne.

Lindsay wiped her face and pointed Midnight at the water jump. Like a perfect gentleman,

Midnight gently obeyed Lindsay's commands. He walked in and stopped in the middle of the water. He stopped because Lindsay was afraid of the bank and he didn't want to scare her.

"Lindsay, you have a very sweet horse," Anne said, trying to cheer her up. "Now if you'll just ask him to walk up that bank, I am sure he will."

Lindsay squeezed her legs around Midnight's sides and he kindly stepped up the two-foot bank.

"Bravo! Bravo! What a good horse!" Anne exclaimed.

Lindsay laughed nervously. She now had just enough confidence to do what Anne asked next. "You see those hay bales half way down the hill? Well, I want you to walk Midnight down to the bottom of the hill, turn around and pick up a trot and take the hay bales."

Lisa didn't like the looks of the hay bale jump because it was sideways on the hill. She walked down to it and strategically stood exactly where she thought Lindsay would fall off if she did.

Lindsay did everything Anne asked but when Midnight jumped, as suspected, Lindsay bobbled

around and fell off just before she got to where her mother was standing. Lindsay fell flat on her back and now cried for good reason. Lisa helped Lindsay up, gave her a hug and grabbed Midnight's reins, who was standing silently by Lindsay's side.

"In all honesty, that was Lindsay's fault; Midnight did fine," Anne said as she approached Lindsay. "Are you all right, Lindsay?"

Lindsay shook her head no. She hunched up her shoulders and gurgled, trying to hold in her tears, but to no avail. "Sweetheart, you really were off balance," Anne said as she wiped Lindsay's cheeks.

On their ride home, Lisa and Lindsay talked all about Anne's hill and how sweet Midnight was and how scary the lesson was.

"I never want to have a lesson there again," Lindsay said.

"Is your back okay?" Lisa asked in concern.

"Well, it hurts."

"I don't think Anne is going to have very good luck giving lessons on that hill. Even the other girl in the lesson had the daylight scared out of her. Carol and Noah did good, but she's been riding for years," Lisa said. "I mean, can you imagine anyone who doesn't know Anne going to her house for a lesson? They would probably faint."

"Tell me about it." Lindsay said, rubbing her back.

"Are you sure you're okay? Do you think I should take you to the hospital?"

Lindsay was exhausted and just shook her head.

Later that night, Anne called to see if Lindsay was okay after her fall. Even though Lindsay was already in bed, Lisa went in and gently nudged her exhausted daughter. "Lindsay, Anne called to see if you're okay," Lisa whispered. "I told her your back hurts, but that I think you will be fine."

Lindsay didn't move.

"RATTLE RATTLE"

Chapter 3

Dead or Alive?

Beau's snake, CoCo, lay in the corner of its cage all curled up in a ball. The red heat lamp shone down on the little snake, warming his body. The heat lamp stayed on 24 hours a day now because the weather had cooled. Beau stared in at his prized possession as he licked his lollipop. Then, while holding the lollipop in his mouth, he carefully reached in the cage and lifted the tiny ball python into his warm hand. Beau gently moved CoCo's body to straighten it out. He walked over to the warm, crackling fire, sat down and quietly studied the slender young snake.

"Mom, CoCo's hungry," Beau said softly and asked, "Can we go get him a pinky?"

Beau's dad, Jeff, had first bought the little tame snake to subside his young son's urge to hunt for wild snakes on their property. The deal was that Jeff would handle everything that the snake needed. Now, Jeff was busier than ever at work and didn't always have time to run to the reptile store to get the snake his weekly meal. "I guess ... if we have to, but we'd better hurry before the store closes," replied Lisa, reluctantly.

"I want to go, too," Jeffrey called.

"Me, too," echoed Lindsay.

Driving to the reptile store, the kids argued and bargained about who would buy the pinky. "Beau is going to buy his snake's food," settled Lisa.

"Can we look around first, Mom?" Jeffrey asked.

"Yes, but just for a little while."

The kids looked at one another with big excited eyes.

Once in the store, they split up and went in all directions. Lindsay liked to look at the teeny, tiny, brightly colored frogs. Jeffrey liked to look at the Komodo dragon, and Beau was drawn to the snake section. Yellow snakes, green snakes, black snakes, big and small, Beau liked them all. Lisa wandered around quietly observing all the strange creatures.

Lisa tapped Beau on the shoulder and directed his attention to the counter, reminding him why they were there. Beau stood in line behind a man ordering two large rats. "Dead or alive?" the teenage girl behind the counter asked the man.

"Alive," he replied.

Lisa and Beau watched as the girl looked in the rat cage for the two biggest rats she could find. She held one up by the tail and asked the man if it was big enough. The man said it was fine and she dropped it down into a card board box. She did the same with the second rat and taped the box shut. The man took his box and left, leaving Beau next in line. "What can I get for you today?" the girl asked Beau.

"I'll have one pinky."

"Dead or alive?" she asked and then shook her head. "Sorry, never mind. I'm just so used to asking that. Pinkies are fine alive." Smiling at Beau, she said, "Oh yeah, you're the boy with the baby Ball. How's it doing?"

"Good," Beau said and smiled a little smile at his mother.

The young girl reached into a rat cage with a big mother rat and ity, bity, teeny, tiny babies all around her. She took one of its brand new babies that were still so new they didn't even have fur, just pink skin and plunked it into a little paper sack and stapled it shut. "That'll be a dollar."

Beau reached into his pocket and pulled out a crinkled one dollar bill his mom had given him and paid for his pinky. "Thank you," he said, carefully taking his sack.

Before they walked away from the counter, Lisa curiously asked the girl, "What do you mean when you say dead or alive?"

Casually, the girl answered, "Some snakes are timid eaters and when they start eating rats, if they don't eat them fast enough, the rats will sometimes bite or scratch the snake. So we kill them first."

Lisa's face contorted when the girl said that. "Believe me; people don't like it when their snakes get hurt."

Lisa continued, "But ... how do you ... you know?"

"Kill 'em?"

"Yeah."

"We wack them," Noticing Lisa's face, she explained, "Really, it's not a big deal. When I first started working here, it did gross me out. I would always have one of the guys kill the food for me. But now I'm so used to it, it just doesn't bother me."

Lisa wanted to ask her how they 'wack' them, but she didn't. "Well, thank you."

All the way home, Beau carefully held the little brown sack. Jeffrey and Lindsay both asked to hold the bag but Beau didn't let them. He knew they would just open it and look in at the little pinky.

Once home, Beau knew the routine. He made a bee line to CoCo's cage, gently lifted the little snake out of his cage, put him in the bag with the pinky, and finally closed the bag. Lindsay, Jeffrey,

Beau and Lisa sat around the little brown bag and waited. They waited and waited and waited and still nothing happened. Jeffrey couldn't wait any more, "Beau, take the snake out of the bag and let him eat the pinky in his cage."

"No, Jeffrey, he likes to eat in the bag," countered Beau.

When still nothing happened, Beau peeked in the bag. CoCo was in a ball and the pinky was lying by his side.

Now Lindsay tried, "Come on, Beau. Take him out of the bag. I bet he'll eat in his cage."

Beau reluctantly took CoCo out of the sack and placed him in his cage. He then placed the pinky right in front the snake.

CoCo's tiny split tongue came out of his mouth and touched the pinky.

"He's smelling it," Lindsay said smartly. "That's how snakes smell, with their tongue."

Round and round CoCo went around the pinky, with his tongue flicking in and out, in and out. Lindsay reached over and moved the pinky by its tiny tail.

"Lindsay! Don't!" Beau exclaimed.

Jeffrey studied the little snake, "Do it again, Lindsay. He's going to eat it."

Lindsay didn't listen to Beau and moved the pinky again. All at once CoCo lunged straight at the little, ity, bity, teeny, tiny pinky and bit it. CoCo held on tight and wrapped his body completely around his prey and squeezed. He squeezed, and he squeezed, and he squeezed, and then he squeezed some more.

"Okay, CoCo, I think you can let go now," Lindsay laughed.

But CoCo didn't let go. He squeezed a little longer and then when he was fully satisfied that he had killed his prey, he slowly unraveled himself and unclamped his jaw, letting go of the pinky. Then, once again, CoCo went around and around, slowly circling and flicking his slender split tongue on his now dead food. CoCo had everyone's undivided attention, and no one spoke. Then the snake opened his mouth, grabbed the pinky's head and clamped down. He swallowed and clamped again. Swallow … clamp … swallow … clamp CoCo repeated, until he had swallowed

the whole pinky and just the tail was hanging out of his mouth.

"He's eating spaghetti now," Beau joked, and everyone breathed a sigh of relief after watching the dramatic show. When CoCo finished his spaghetti, Beau picked him up.

"Beau, you can't play with him now, remember. He has to digest," Lindsay reminded.

"I know," Beau said, placing CoCo back in his cage under his heat lamp for him to digest his weekly meal. While resting under warm heat, CoCo yawned.

"How cute, he's tired," Lisa said.

Lindsay corrected her mother, "No, he's getting his jaw back in place. They do that after they eat. I read it in Beau's snake book."

"Oh. Well he looks like he's yawning."

Throughout the whole snake feeding episode, Cheyenne, the family's long-haired red dachshund, sat strangely attentive. Since moving to the country, Cheyenne had discovered her true hunting instincts. At the young age of three, she now knew exactly what it meant to be a scent hound. A single whiff of rat would change her from a sweet house dog into a relentless hunter. She sat with her chest puffed out and just the tops of her long ears pricked slightly up. "Mom, I think Cheyenne thinks there's a rat in the house," noticed Jeffrey. Cheyenne quivered. The kids laughed and Cheyenne quivered again. Her long nose pointed straight at the little brown bag the pinky had been in. "She must smell the rat scent. Give her the bag," Lisa suggested.

Cheyenne happily sniffed the sack and without a moment's hesitation, pounced on it.

She pounced and sniffed and scratched and chewed until she had the little sack shredded into small pieces all over the floor. She sniffed and checked each little piece of paper making doubly

"Sniff Sniff"

sure there was no rat in the house. Everyone laughed at Cheyenne's enthusiasm and each week thereafter, not only did CoCo get a meal, but Cheyenne got the privilege of destroying the rat bag.

Chapter 4

Barbed Wire

One Saturday morning, Lindsay, Jeffrey and Beau went outside to visit Midnight. Jeff and Lisa were talking at the breakfast table and discussing Anne's hill and how Lindsay should start having lessons on their own property. Suddenly, all three kids ran into the house shouting, "Moon's missing!"

Jeff immediately stood up and looked out the big picture window in the living room that overlooked the whole front half of their property. "Are you sure?"

"Yeah, Dad," Beau said, who had a firm grip on Cheyenne's leash.

"His corral gate is wide open!" Jeffrey exclaimed, breathing hard.

"And *believe* me," exclaimed Lindsay dramatically, "he is *not* in his corral!"

Lisa hurriedly put on her tennis shoes and quickly walked outside. Sure enough, Moon was not in his corral, nor anywhere to be seen.

"Mom, I am going to check on Midnight!" Lindsay said running off up the hill to his corral.

Jeff began to complain, "We're responsible for that horse, and if he gets out on the road and—"

"Mom, Dad," Lindsay hollered from the top of the hill. "Moon is up here with Midnight."

Jeffrey and Beau looked at each other for a minute with their eyes big, and began to walk up the hill. Sugar, the Wrights' guard dog purchased as a puppy just a year earlier stood in between the boys panting and wagging her tail. She looked at Jeffrey and then at Beau, waiting to see what would happen next.

"Come on, Sugar," called Jeffrey. Sugar

energetically and obediently followed Jeffrey's command.

"Come on Cheyenne," echoed Beau giving a little tug on her leash.

Lisa walked up the hill to see what was going on, and when she got to Midnight's corral, she saw Moon and Midnight basking in the morning sunlight together. No stampede, no nervousness, no broken fence, no nothing.

"Lindsay, was he in the corral when you got up here, or did you put him in the corral with Midnight?" Lisa asked with a puzzled look on her face.

"No, this is exactly where he was when I saw him," Lindsay assured her mother.

"I don't understand. How did he get in there if no one opened the gate and let him in?" Lisa asked, looking around for evidence.

"Maybe he jumped in, Mom," offered Beau.

Lisa walked around the old corral and inspected the old swaying cables and the leaning railroad ties. As she got around to the far end of the corral, which was the only section of the corral that had barbed wire remaining, she had her answer. "Oh my gosh, he busted right through the barbed wire, all three strands!" Lisa quickly went to Moon and checked him over for the cuts she knew he would have. "I can't believe it! I can hardly find a scratch on him. You guys, come here!" Lisa showed the kids the barbed wire, which was camouflaged by the big tumbleweeds that surrounded it, and then she had them look at Moon's chest, where there was only one teeny, tiny, little scratch.

"Why did Moon do that?" Jeffrey asked.

"I have no idea. I guess he wants to live in Midnight's corral with him," Lisa replied.

"He probably didn't see the barbed wire because of all the weeds," Jeffrey said knowingly.

"Can Moon just stay in this corral now?" Beau asked.

"For now," Lisa agreed.

"Mom, remember, Anne said not to have them in the same corral," reminded Lindsay.

"I know, but I certainly don't want Moon escaping again and breaking back into Midnight's corral. Anyway, look how happy they are together and Moon has a lot more space to run around in."

"Okay, but I'll say 'I told you so' if something happens," Lindsay announced.

Lisa started realizing just how much she didn't know about horses and horse behavior. She had so many questions and no answers. Why couldn't she control Moon? Why does he always buck? Why does he bob his head? Why does he practically walk on top of her when she leads him? Why does he calm down on the trail when Midnight is next to him? Why did Midnight pull back and break the fence? Why did Moon break into Midnight's corral? Why did Anne say not to put them in together? Why did Anne say to put oil on their feed? "You know what we are going to do today, kids?"

"What?" they asked in unison.

"We are going to the library. Yep," Lisa said trying to convince herself of what she knew she needed to do. "We are definitely going to the library."

As they all began to walk back down to the

house, they realized that Sugar had disappeared. "Sugar … Sugar," the kids called.

"Oh my gosh, Mom, Sugar is in the horses' water tub," Lindsay laughed.

Sugar seemed to think it was funny, too. The corners of her mouth were turned up, as if she was smiling as she continued soaking in the tub. When the kids called her again, she gently stepped out of the tub with her front feet first, then awkwardly brought her back legs out one by one. When Lisa said, "You are a silly dog," Sugar playfully ran around with water dripping off her, and then suddenly tucked her head down and somersaulted into the dirt. She rolled on one side and then the other until she was completely caked in dirt. Lisa and the children laughed at Sugar's antics, and the more they laughed, the more Sugar goofed off. She stood up and began to hop around in circles faster and faster she went until she fell in a heap on accident, but acting as if she did it on purpose, like that was the way she wanted her show to end. As Lisa and the kids laughed, Sugar suddenly stood up and gazed out over the

property. She stood bravely and boldly as the hair on her back began to rise up.

"Sugar, what do you see, girl?" Lisa asked.

Sugar crouched down and growled under her breath. She was a big dog now, and still fine-tuning her guarding instincts.

"Mom, I don't think she sees anything," Lindsay said.

"Ya wanna bet, Lindsay?" Jeffrey countered. pointing to a big coyote crossing the property.

Cheyenne stuck her long nose up in the air and sniffed the wind. Her small brown eyes couldn't see what her highly tuned nose smelled. Cheyenne began to bark. "Sniff, sniff, bark, bark," she went.

"Beau, keep hold of Cheyenne," Lisa said seriously.

Sugar had never seen a coyote, but she instinctively didn't like it. Sugar looked at Cheyenne and decided that she should bark, too. Unafraid, the coyote stopped and stared up the hill to see the barking dogs. In her crouched down position, Sugar began to creep closer.

Strategically barking and creeping, barking and creeping, Sugar went until the coyote moved on. When Sugar had seen the last of the strange, scrappy animal, she ran victoriously back to her family. "Good girl, Sugar!" cried Lindsay.

"Oh, good girl Shoogy!" echoed Jeffrey, trying to pat down the Mohawk on her back.

"It's a good thing that we have Sugar, huh, Mom? That coyote could eat Cheyenne, huh, Mom?" Beau commented as he held Cheyenne in his arms the rest of the way down the hill.

Lisa agreed, "Yes, Beau, it's a very good thing that we have Sugar."

"Why didn't I think of this sooner?" Lisa whispered to herself as she stood gazing at all of the horse books in an isle of the little local library. She picked one and then another, then another and another until she couldn't hold anymore.

When Lindsay saw her mother with her arms full of books, she laughed, "Gee, Mom, like you can really read all of those?"

The librarian said, "There's a library rule that

only six books per subject can be checked out at one time, so you'll have to put some back." Lindsay, Jeffrey and Beau stood and watched their Mom examine every book and try to make up her mind which six she would check out.

"Mom, come on, just get some and let's go," Jeffrey said impatiently.

"I'm going to the car," Lindsay said, not understanding how it could take her mother so long to pick out a few books. Lindsay never had any trouble making up her mind. Beau followed Lindsay outside and Lisa quickly made her choice including one book on coyotes.

That day was the true beginning of what would be a year-long study of horses and horse behavior, not only for Lisa who was reading the books, but also for the whole family. Whenever she found an interesting fact or bit of information, she couldn't help but let everyone know.

"Honey, can we not talk about horses anymore, at least for the rest of dinner?" Jeff requested one evening.

"Honey, all I'm saying is that Anne was

wrong about telling us to keep the horses separate. Horses are herd animals; that's why Moon broke into Midnight's corral. It's their instinct to be together and, in the wild, they stick together for protection. As a matter of fact, if a group of horses doesn't like a particular horse, they'll exclude that horse from the herd for punishment. Then the horse becomes nervous and afraid because it's now more likely to be attacked by a wild animal." Lisa paused to take a sip of water and then continued, "So really, if you think about it, by keeping Moon and Midnight apart, we were punishing them both."

Jeff looked at the kids as they listened intently to the latest bit of information. "Honey, that's great. Now can we please change the subject?"

"Well, I'm just saying, it's just kind of sad, you know. Horses have nothing to defend themselves with except their legs to run with. That's why horses are such frightful animals; they have to be to survive. If they hear a rattle in the bush, they don't have time to wait around and find out what it is, they run first, then when they are at a safe distance, they turn around to see what it was."

Suddenly the kids got involved with the conversation. "Why would a big horse be afraid of a little rattle in a bush?" Jeffrey asked.

Jeff nodded with his mouth full and then tried to speak, "Yeah, honey, tell him why a big horse would be afraid of a little rattle in a bush."

Lisa smiled at Jeff and then answered the question. "Jeffrey, for all the horse knows, the rattle could be a big lion crouched down waiting to pounce on his back and have him for dinner."

"Could a lion really eat a whole horse?" asked Beau.

"No, Beau," Lindsay said smartly, "but the lion's whole family could."

Lisa went on, "That's why racehorses are usually more high-strung than other horses that haven't raced. Because they have been trained to run, and one reason horses run is out of fear. So during a race, if a jockey uses his whip, for all the horse knows, the sting he feels could be a lion's claw which he never fully gets away from."

"Then why doesn't Midnight get scared?" asked Lindsay .

"First of all, Midnight wasn't raced. Second of all, he is more mature and wise, and lastly, he was trained to listen to his rider. You see, horses don't want to be afraid anymore than you or I want to be afraid, so I need to work on building my trust with Moon and getting him to listen to me. If I tell him to calm down, then he should calm down. If I tell him things are fine, then he needs to learn that things are fine. But, you can never a hundred percent get rid of a horse's spooking instinct, nor would you want to. But you can train them to be obedient to you."

"I bet I can get Midnight to be a hundred percent spook-free," Lindsay said.

"So, if Midnight was standing under one of our big pepper trees and a big branch decided to suddenly break, would you want Midnight to run out from the tree or stand there dumb as a door nail?"

Lindsay smiled, "Umm … run?"

"Exactly," Lisa smirked.

Jeff had heard enough, "I don't know about you, but for all this horse knows, is that I need a big bowl of vanilla ice cream." The kids laughed, they liked it when their dad ate ice cream because that was the only time they were allowed to have it.

Once everyone was quietly enjoying their ice cream, Lisa couldn't help herself, "You know, they say that a horse becomes a mirror of his master's mood and personality."

"So you're saying that Moon will develop your mood and your personality? Great, I can hardly wait to have a horse that acts like my wife," Jeff joked.

"Funny, very funny. No, that's not what I'm saying. I'm saying that maybe if I am calm and assured when I am around Moon, then he will become calm and assured. Anyway, you're not the one who rides him. Some of his spooks and bucks are life-threatening. Just ask Lindsay."

"It's true, Dad. Moon bucks really high and when he spooks, he jumps sideways really fast."

"Thank you very much, Lindsay," said Lisa, patting her daughter's arm.

"Well, you need to be careful when you ride him. He is definitely not your average horse, I saw that in him the day I bought him. He's a champ, you know, a true champ. He's got the 'eye of the tiger.'"

Even though Jeff didn't ride Moon, he loved the horse; he loved his competitive nature and the look in his eye. Lisa stared at Jeff with a funny look as he went on about Moon and then he caught on, "I know what you are thinking, I'm not afraid of Moon, not one bit and I'm not afraid to ride him. I'm just too busy. I'll ride him one day, you just wait. I will definitely ride him."

Chapter 5

The Wig Deal

"Mom, do you really think Dad is going to like the saddle?" Lindsay asked.

"I hope so. Anyway, now he won't have an excuse to not ride."

"I bet he's going to be mad that you spent so much money."

"Dad always says, you get what you pay for," Lisa said in justification.

Lindsay was right, if there was one thing her dad disliked, it was surprises. Lisa was aware of that, but the saddle was of such fine quality that she couldn't pass it up. She was sure Jeff would like it when he saw the fine workmanship, the detailed tooling in the rich brown leather, and the decorative silver trim.

"Mom, was that man grouchy?" Beau asked.

Lisa laughed, "Yes, very grouchy. I almost didn't want to buy anything from him because he was so grouchy. And all of his prices were too high."

"I think you should have bought the English saddle," Lindsay observed.

"I don't know why we had to buy any saddle at all," Jeffrey added.

As usual, right when the kids saw their dad, they went right on ahead and told him about the saddle.

"I thought we had two saddles already. Why would we need another one," Jeff asked, a sour look on his face. Lisa took him to the van to show him the saddle, and watched him closely, trying to read his mind, as he looked it over. "I'll tell you right now that Moon will not want that saddle on his back."

Jeff picked the saddle up in his arms and, lifting it up and down, guessed its weight. "This saddle must weigh fifty pounds or more. How much did it cost?

I never said I needed a saddle," Jeff said, setting the saddle back down and walking into the house.

The next day when Lisa put the saddle on Moon, she realized that she had made a mistake. The saddle was way too big for Moon's back. Moon was narrow and the saddle was wide. She tried another pad, and then another until she knew it would never work. The big western saddle looked ridiculous on Moons narrow frame.

Lisa told Jeff about the saddle not fitting and that she would try to return it. But when she did, the grouchy man told her no, he would not take the saddle back.

Lisa gently broke the news to Jeff, "Honey, I'm sorry, but the man said he won't give me my check back. He said, 'A deal is a deal.'"

"No, a deal is not a deal until the deal is over, and the deal is not over. Now both of us are going to return this saddle before the day is over."

Jeff knocked on the man's door and waited and waited, he knocked again until finally the grouchy man opened up the door. He was

grouchier than ever and wearing his pajamas. "Hi, sir," Jeff started. "My wife bought this saddle yesterday, but it doesn't seem to fit our horse. I'm sure you would understand if we wanted our check back."

"I told her a deal is a deal. The saddle is yours now, so if you don't want it, sell it yourself."

"But, sir …." Round and round Jeff went until finally the saddle was returned.

All the way home, Lisa listened to Jeff, "Okay, look, I got you out of this one, but don't go buying anything else. Money is a little tight right now."

Over the next few weeks, Lindsay and her mother rode often and Lisa began to notice that Lindsay was beginning to stretch out. "Lindsay, have you been growing? You look like you've outgrown your little saddle."

"I think so, my knees don't really fit on my knee rolls anymore," Lindsay said.

"Maybe we should get you a bigger saddle."

"I told you we should have gotten that man's English saddle," Lindsay said.

"Yep, you were right. Hey, maybe ... no—" Lisa started and stopped quickly.

"What?"

"Maybe that grouchy man still has that English saddle for sale."

If only Lisa could get Jeff to agree ... If only she could get Jeff to see that Lindsay needed that English saddle the grouchy man had sitting in his garage.

"Are you crazy!?" Jeff yelled.

"Honey, you don't have to yell, it's really hard to find a good saddle, and I know for a fact that the man's English saddle would fit both Moon and Midnight and Lindsay. It was a really good brand and it cost less than his western saddle," Lisa explained.

"And you're going to face that man again? I bet he wouldn't even open the door if he saw you coming," added Jeff with a laugh.

"Can we afford it then? I am telling you, Lindsay really needs a bigger saddle."

"If you think she really needs it, go ahead and call the man to see if he still has it, but I'm out of it. I will *not* be going back and forth on this one."

Lisa telephoned the man but when he answered in a cranky tone of voice, she choked. Sudden fear gripped her throat and nothing came out. "Hello? Hello?" the cranky voice called.

Then she had an idea, "Well hello, sir, um, my name is … uh … Ginny," she whispered in a soft southern accent, "I was a'wondren if you still have your English saddle for sale?"

"Yes, ma'am, I do," the man answered cordially.

Lisa continued in her suddenly new voice, "That's mighty fine, sir, and if you don't mind, I would rightly like to come and take a look at it." Lisa let the man give her directions again even though she already knew where he lived.

When she hung up the phone, Jeff was staring right at her. "If I didn't hear it for myself, I wouldn't have believed it. So, *Ginny,* I don't know what you're up to, but like I said, you're on your own. Got it…*Ginny?*" Jeff said, laughing.

Lisa ran to the bathroom and looked at herself in the mirror. She twisted her hair up one way and then the other and put on her reading glasses. Jeff watched her and shook his head in disbelief. "He's going to know it's you. You still look the same except your hair is in a bun and you have glasses on."

Lisa took another look at herself. "You're right," she said nervously. Jeff had seen enough and walked out of the room. Lisa began to rummage through her closet trying on different hats and scarves, until she ran across a black wig. She pinned up her long blonde hair, pulled the jet-black wig down snuggly over her head making sure that not a single strand of blonde showed, then added her glasses for an extra security measure. Now satisfied with the transformation she saw in the mirror, she smiled and greeted herself, "Hello, Ginny," and giggled.

She grabbed her purse, and was heading for the door, when the kids caught sight of her.

Jeffrey laughed, "Hey, look at Mom!"

Lindsay had her eyes wide open and blinking slow dramatic blinks. With a slight smile forming on her open mouth, she asked, "Mom, *where* are you going with that black wig on?"

Jeff stared in disbelief at his wife with black hair. "Look kids," he started somberly, "I am sorry to say that your mom is not normal."

The kids and Jeff laughed. "She's going to buy a saddle," Jeff said, still laughing.

When Lisa walked outside, Sugar barked and Cheyenne wagged her tail at the stranger. "Quiet, you guys, it's me."

Lisa drove nervously to the old man's house, now for the fourth time, checking her wig often in the rear view mirror and continually tucking in a stubborn piece of blonde hair. When the man let her in to look at the saddle, Lisa tried her best to talk real southern, "Boy, that's a mighty fine saddle," she said and continued in her accent, "I'll bet you were a great rider."

For the first time, the old man smiled, "Well, I guess you could say that."

Lisa was surprised to see another side of the grouchy man, so she continued, "I'll bet you rode real spirited horses." The man smiled again and nodded. All Lisa really wanted was to buy the English saddle and get out of there without him noticing that it was the same lady who wrecked the western saddle deal. Lisa carefully examined the English saddle, making doubly sure that it was worth it.

The man watched and waited and before Lisa said a thing, the now not so grouchy man said, "Ma'am, seeing that you're a southern lady, I'm going to knock a hundred dollars off the price of the saddle. I know people from the south like a good deal."

Lisa stood up and adjusted her glasses, "Well sir, that's a mighty generous offer," she said softly, "I'd be a fool not to take it." Lisa handed the man cash this time and the deal was done.

Chapter 6

A Cloud of Dust

Jeff looked funny brushing a horse. He didn't do it like Lindsay or Lisa, who took their time. Instead, he did it quickly, as if he was in a hurry. For some reason, he seemed to treat everything like a business. "Come on, Moon. Stand still, so we can get this job done," he said as he shook off the pad and laid it on Moon's back. Then, like he'd been doing it his whole life, he put the saddle on and loosely buckled the girth. After bridling Moon, he finished up by tightened the girth as tight as he could. Moon put his ears back slightly and wrinkled his nose.

"Um, Dad, I don't think you should make Moon's girth that tight," advised Lindsay.

"Lindsay, my grandpa taught me how to saddle a horse, and he said the last thing you want is a loose girth. I remember him girthing up his horses, and he made sure that the girth was good and tight," Jeff said, checking the girth and putting it up one more notch, just to be on the safe side.

Lindsay raised her eyebrows but kept her mouth shut; she didn't want to take a chance on spoiling their first ride together. "There," Jeff said wiping the sweat from his brow as he led Moon by his bridle out the corral gate.

As Jeff raised his leg to put his foot in the stirrup, Lindsay spoke up. "Dad, Mom doesn't do it like that. She says that you should use a chair or a tree stump or something to help you get up so you don't put so much pressure on his wither."

"What's a wither?" Jeff asked cautiously.

Lindsay laughed, "It's that boney thing in front of the saddle. Mom says it's sensitive."

"Oh, well, this is how my grandpa taught me to get on a horse and that's how I'm going to get

"Steady Moon"

on. He said you always get on from the left side and you use your stirrup."

"Go ahead and try then," Lindsay said with a slight shake of her head.

Again, Jeff raised his leg and just when he got his foot in the stirrup, Moon began to walk forward impatiently. "Hey, what's he doing? Whoa!" he called, hopping on one foot.

Lindsay bent over Midnight's neck and had a good laugh, "Dad, he doesn't know how to stand still."

"Well, he's going to learn right now then," Jeff said stubbornly refusing to take Lindsay's advice. Lindsay waited and watched as her Dad went round and round with Moon about standing still until he finally mounted Moon the way his grandpa had taught him. "There! All this horse needs is a man to ride him and he'll be fine."

On their way walking down the hill, they stopped at the house to talk to Lisa and Grandma who was over visiting.

Grandma smiled at Jeff riding Moon, "You sure have their coats shining," she said and added,

"Lindsay, it looks like Midnight is a real sweet horse."

"He is, Grandma. Watch what he does when I pet him on his neck." Lindsay stroked Midnight's neck and told him he was a good boy. Right on cue, Midnight licked his lips, comforted by Lindsay's words.

Grandma tilted her head to one side and smiled, "Oh, how sweet. He likes it when you do that," she said as she gently straightened a few strands of Midnight's forelock.

"Clippity clop, clippity clop," went the horses' hooves as father and daughter went down the long driveway on their very first trail ride together. Lisa was glad her mother was there to witness it. She was proud at that moment, proud that she had married a man who would ride a horse with his daughter. Lisa watched them until they disappeared into the orange groves.

While Jeff and Lindsay were gone, Grandma, Lisa and the boys were outside enjoying the weather, although when Lisa heard a faint scream from a far off distance, she panicked. "Was that

Lindsay?" She ran around to the front of the house where she'd heard the scream come from. Lisa heard thundering hooves running up the hill, but all she could see was a cloud of dust. Something was definitely wrong. Had Lindsay fallen? Had Midnight bucked her off? Lisa chased the cloud of dust as fast as she could. What she found was not what she expected. There, before her, was Jeff stretched out flat on his back not moving a muscle with dirt all over his face and clothes. Sugar and Cheyenne made it to Jeff first and began to lick him all over his face and he still didn't move. He for sure wasn't faking because he never let the dogs lick him in the face.

"Honey! Are you okay?" Lisa said as she jostled him. Jeff just moaned and moved his legs a little, and then he spit trying to get the dirt out of his mouth. Sugar and Cheyenne wagged their tail as they continued licking him in the face. They thought it was funny that Jeff was letting them lick him. "Honey, what happened? Where's Lindsay?" she asked. Jeff spit again and moaned some more and tried to open his dirt-filled eyes.

"Huh? What did you say?" Jeff moaned.

"I said, what happened? Are you okay?"

Jeff lifted his legs and acted as if he was going to get up, but then collapsed flat on his back. "I'm okay, just go get Moon," he moaned.

Having no idea where Lindsay was, Lisa began to follow the cloud of dust that was still lingering in the air. As she approached the top of the hill, she could hear Lindsay talking in the distance, "Lindsay!"

"I'm in the orange grove, Mom."

Lisa walked toward her daughter's voice through the thick forest of trees. "Where?"

"Here!"

Closer and closer Lisa got to the voice. "Where?"

"I'm over here, holding Moon."

Lisa was relieved to find her daughter safe. "What happened?" she asked, taking Moon's one rein from Lindsay.

"Moon bucked Dad off sky high!" Lindsay explained excitedly as they walked out of the orange grove. "I saw the whole thing, Mom.

When I saw Dad fall, I rode Midnight over to check on him because I know that old people's bones are fragile and everything, and I wanted to make sure he didn't break anything. Dad said he was fine and told me to go get Moon. So," Lindsay paused for a breath, "I ran Midnight as fast as I could to catch Moon. I was really nervous when I saw him run in the orange groves, but I knew that I had to catch him. Luckily he stopped right here and I grabbed his one rein. The other one broke."

"Yeah, I see that," said Lisa. "Are you okay?"

Lindsay was excited and breathing hard, "Oh yeah," she said dramatically, "I'm fine, but I don't know about Dad."

"I think Dad is going to be fine, but he's going to be awfully sore."

Lisa and Lindsay quickly put the horses away and walked back to the house. Lindsay continued talking about her Dad and Moon's buck, adding a good amount of drama.

"Lindsay, you know how I found Dad?"

"How?" she wondered.

"I found Dad at the bottom of the hill, lying flat on his back covered in dirt, with Sugar and Cheyenne licking him in the face."

Lindsay giggled, "Oh, Gosh! I know why Moon bucked Dad off, Mom."

"You do?"

"He tightened Moon's girth way too tight. I told him it was too tight, but he said that's the way his grandpa did it. And you know how Moon hates a tight girth!"

"Yes. Moon hates a lot of things."

Lindsay laughed again, "Mom, you should have seen it. Moon's back legs were straight up in the air and Dad seriously went flying!"

Jeff had somehow made his way back in the house and Jeffrey and Beau had made an icepack for his head.

Lisa hated to see Jeff hurt, but when she saw him laying stretched out on the couch with an ice pack on his head, and after all the things he said about Moon and how he is a champ and all, she couldn't help laughing. She covered her mouth and plugged her nose in an attempt to hold in her laughter but when she did, it sounded like she was blowing her nose.

"I hear you," Jeff moaned, with the icepack covering his eyes. "Go ahead, laugh. I know you're laughing."

Lisa walked into the kitchen to try to compose herself and found Grandma busy making another icepack. Concealing a slight smile, Grandma whispered, "Is he okay? Gosh, I forgot how dangerous horses can be."

"I think he'll be fine," Lisa said.

The boys didn't like seeing their dad incapacitated and they certainly didn't like not hearing him talk, so they began drilling him with questions. "Why did you fall off, Dad?" Beau asked.

"Maybe you should have held on tighter," Jeffrey said.

"Did you fall on your stomach or your back?" asked Beau.

"Are you going to ride Moon again?" Jeffrey asked.

"Do you need a Band-Aid?" Beau offered.

"Do you want a blanket, Dad?" asked Jeffrey.

"Do you want a pillow?" Beau asked.

Jeff didn't answer one of their questions, but just moaned and said, "Bath. Run a hot bath for me." Jeffrey and Beau ran down the hallway to start running the bath.

From that day on, Jeff was different. Moon had changed him, humbled him in a way that no man could. He had a new respect for horses, especially Moon. After all, Moon was different. Jeff still liked that about him. He saw something in Moon that he saw in himself and he accepted that. And, now he really believed Lisa when she would tell him about her escapades with Moon. Jeff was sore for a long time, but there were no lasting injuries ... except maybe to his ego. Jeff didn't want anyone outside the family to know what happened ... at least not for a long, long, time.

Chapter 7

The Bad, Bad Kick

December turned out to be a cold, cold month. At night when the temperature dropped to freezing or below, giant wind machines in the orange groves would automatically turn on and blow the frigid air out of the groves. The fan motors would hum and rumble all night long as they saved an entire crop from ruin. The big, bright, juicy oranges that had been cared for all year long would soon be picked.

Picking season was an active time in Windsor Heights. Buses, tractors, forklifts, crates, and pickers lined the roads and groves. The pickers carried ladders and cloth sacks slung over one shoulder to collect the oranges in. The pickers happily scattered through the groves, leaning their ladders right up against the orange trees. The tips of their ladders extended upward and ended in the sky.

Little by little, the pickers worked their way through the forest of trees next to the Wright's house and on upward toward the horse corrals. They couldn't be seen, but their singing carried over the tops of the trees and their ladders mysteriously moved about through the sky. Picking and singing, the pickers went for a week straight. Crates and crates of beautiful, sweet oranges were loaded onto big trucks ready to take to citrus packing houses, and then to markets all over the country.

All during picking season, Sugar and Cheyenne barked and barked in the house, and Moon carried on watching and snorting at the mysterious ladders moving about through the trees. Midnight wasn't bothered by the pickers; he had seen them year after

year and was used to them. What did bother Midnight, however, was Moon. Moon would rant and rave and run about, bumping into Midnight, trying to get the old horse to run and be scared with him. Sometimes, Midnight would reluctantly give in to Moon's wishes and run around the corral once or twice with him.

One late, particularly chilly afternoon, Lisa, Lindsay, Jeffrey and Beau were up with the horses when Moon was having one of his temper tantrums. His coat seemed to be filled with electricity as he ran and bucked, and then reared and bucked some more. Midnight tried to mind his own business but Moon wouldn't let him. Moon insisted Midnight play his game. Moon bumped Midnight and reared right in front of his face. When Midnight refused to move, Moon turned and ran away with a buck.

"What was that?" Lisa asked. "Did you hear that?"

"I think he kicked Midnight in the knee," Lindsay said.

Lisa panicked at what she saw next. Midnight was frozen with fear, his ears falling half way down from their usual upright position. And he stuck his left front leg straight out in front of him, holding it slightly off the ground. Lisa and Lindsay ran to Midnight to see what had happened. Midnight trembled and acted as if he was going fall down. Lisa bent down to get a good look at Midnight's knee. It was split clean down to the bone and blood was spurting out. "Oh gosh, Lindsay, what do we do?" Lisa asked fretfully.

"Let's call Dr. Vered."

"Wait, maybe we can fix him. At least let's try to stop the bleeding," Lisa said, confused as she noticed a small pool of blood forming on the ground.

Lindsay stroked Midnight on the neck and spoke gentle words of comfort to him, "Oh Midnight, you're going to be okay, I promise."

Lisa looked back at the boys, who were both silently staring from the edge of the corral. "Jeffrey, I need you to take Beau back down to the house before it gets dark. Midnight is hurt and I have to see if I can help him." Jeffrey immediately grabbed Beau's hand and walked his little brother safely back to the house.

Meanwhile, Lisa and Lindsay began rummaging through their meager first aid supplies. Midnight couldn't move, so they tried their best to doctor him in the corral. First, they wrapped a towel snuggly around his knee to stop the bleeding. Lisa felt better now that she couldn't see the wound. She held the towel firmly in place while she caught her breath and tried to think of what to do next.

"Mom, maybe we should call Anne."

Lisa silently shook her head, "Lindsay, she's the one who told us not to put these two horses in the same corral. I can't call her."

"Well, can't we call Dr. Vered?" Lindsay suggested in distress.

"It's late, Lindsay, and I doubt if he'll even be able to come at this time." Lisa took a deep breath and slowly blew it out, focusing back on Midnight's wound. She slowly lifted the towel off his knee and was relieved to see that most of the bleeding had stopped. "Hand me the gauze and tape," she asked Lindsay. Lisa gently laid a square piece of gauze over the cut and rolled some extra gauze around and around Midnight's knee and taped it securely in place.

Midnight still didn't want to move, so Lindsay brought his dinner bucket to him and placed it right under his nose. Midnight sniffed and then nibbled at his food. Nothing else could be done.

That night during dinner, the kids explained to their dad what happened to Midnight. Jeff stopped eating and looked straight at Lisa, "Did you call Dr. Vered?"

"No," Lisa answered with a fretful tone of voice.

"Why am I the last one to find out about things

that go on around here?" Jeff said, getting up from the table. He picked up the phone and started dialing. When no one answered, he left a message. "Hey, Doc, it's Jeff Wright. We just had a horse here kick another horse in the knee and I think you might need to come out and take a look at it." Jeff hung up the phone and sat back down at the table.

"Honey, I don't actually know if Dr. Vered can do anything to help Midnight."

"Well, from now on, I need to know when something happens like this. If he was called earlier, we might have been able to reach him."

Lindsay chimed in, "I told Mom that we should call him."

Jeffrey tried to change the subject, "Dad, Moon bucks really high and when he bucks, he ..." Jeffrey started laughing. "Well, when he bucks, he ..." Jeffrey laughed again which made Beau laugh.

Lindsay giggled, "I know what you're going to say. Every time Moon bucks, he ..." now all three children had the giggles and their faces were red.

"You guys. Don't say what I think you're going to say while we're at the dinner table," Lisa commanded.

Jeff looked confused, "What does Moon do when he bucks?"

Lindsay, Jeffrey and Beau were in such a state of hysteria they couldn't answer so Lisa did her best to politely explain, "Moon has ...." Now Lisa laughed and couldn't quite spit out what she wanted to say.

Lindsay fanned herself with her napkin and dried her eyes from the tears of laughter shooting from her eyes, "Dad, Moon has gas."

Jeff shook his head at the children's silliness, "I told you, he's not your average horse."

The next day Dr. Vered made a trip to the Wright's home to have a look at Midnight's knee. After examining the horse's leg wound, Dr. Vered stood up and gave his diagnosis to Lisa and Jeff, "Well, it definitely appears that Midnight was kicked hard, but the wound has already begun to heal closed. The knee area is a hard place to put stitches because when they bend their knee it tends to pull the stitches out. I think it's best to let him heal Indian style."

That got Lisa's attention. "What's Indian style?"

"Basically we say Indian style when we just let a wound heal naturally. He's going to be sore for a while, but he should recover eventually. You can ice his knee or run a cold hose on it to relieve any swelling," he said, closing his bag and making his way back to his van.

Midnight was sore and walked with a limp for weeks following his bad, bad kick. Lisa was sorry that Midnight was hurt, and sorry for Lindsay that she couldn't ride her horse on her first Christmas with him. But injured or not, Midnight would be in the Wright family's Christmas card.

One day, Lisa thought, *It wouldn't hurt Midnight if Lindsay sat on him just for a moment, a quick moment.* So Lisa lifted Lindsay up on Midnight's back and had Jeffrey and Beau stand in front of him while she focused her camera, "Smile, say Merry Christmas!"

"Merry Christmas!"

Chapter 8

Showing Midnight

Lisa never wanted Anne to find out about Midnight's injury, but when she called to set up lessons for Lindsay, Lisa confessed, "Anne, Lindsay won't be able to have lessons for a while."

"Oh, why?" Anne asked.

"Midnight was kicked by Moon and he is completely lame."

"Were they in the same corral?"

"Yes, Anne, I am afraid so," Lisa started and continued as she recounted the details of the incident, "It was pretty bad. I thought Midnight was going to fall down, his ears dropped and everything."

Anne graciously explained, "That's called shock, sweetheart. He was in shock. Why didn't you call me? I could have helped you."

"I was embarrassed because you warned me about letting the horses share a corral. I just thought they liked being together"

Anne tried to make Lisa feel better, "Oh they do like being together, but it's times like these that make it not worth it. But please call me next time. Believe me, I've seen everything."

"So do you think Midnight will get better?"

"Yes. Don't worry. I promise Midnight will get better."

It was spring now, and as Anne had promised, Midnight fully recovered. Lindsay couldn't wait to get home from school. Tapping her knee impatiently, she rolled down her window to let her hot face blow in the wind. She had everything planned out in her head that she needed to do when she got home. Her mother always said, "I don't ask for too much when you get home, just the basics. Wash your hands, drink your water, straighten your room and get your homework and piano done."

The worst of everything was the water. Lindsay hated drinking so much water, but her mom said, "It's good for your skin and living in Riverside is like living in a desert, so you need to drink a lot."

As soon as they pulled into their driveway, Lindsay flung open her door and lugged her heavy backpack into the sunroom, where she dropped it in a heap. She quickly washed her hands and ran to be first on the piano. As Lindsay began practicing, her mother called, "Lindsay, did you have your water?" Lindsay stopped what she was doing and went in the kitchen to have a glass of water. Her mother watched her drink it, so she couldn't pour any of it down the sink and then back to the piano she went. Lickity split, her fingers flew over the piano keys. She and her brothers didn't really want to play the piano, but their mom always said, "It's part of your education and until you've practiced, you can't do anything else."

After playing the piano, Lindsay dug through her backpack and got out her schoolwork. That was the easiest for Lindsay because she liked doing schoolwork and getting good grades. She liked to hear her mom and dad talk about how on earth they had a daughter that got such good grades. As soon as Lindsay finished her homework, she went to her room and changed into her riding clothes and then out the door she went.

"Oh, Lindsay," called her mother waving her back to the house. "Did you get your room straightened?"

"Whoops!" Lindsay said, walking back into the house.

"That's what I thought, and it had better get done the right way. If I find anything squashed in your drawers or thrown in your closet, you'll do it all over the right way, understand?"

"Yes ...," Lindsay said in a drawn out, exasperated tone.

Actually, Lindsay didn't know what was worse, drinking so much water, or straightening her room. No one including Lindsay knew how her room got so messy so fast. Her dad said it looked as if a bomb had gone off in her room, and her mom said that her brothers could go a whole week sharing their room and it wouldn't get as messy as her room did in one day. Lindsay would just close her door, turn on her radio and think about Midnight. If she thought real hard about Midnight when she was putting her clothes away, then before she knew it, her room was straight.

"Can I go get Midnight out now, Mom?" asked Lindsay, "I did my homework and piano, straightened my room and everything."

Lisa was helping Beau with his piano, "Count out loud, Beau. One, two, three … one, two, three …." She looked at Lindsay and nodded her head. On her way out, Lindsay put two carrots and two apples in a sack to take up to the corrals.

Walking up the big hill to the horses made Lindsay breathe hard, so she kept her head down and pretended she was walking on flat ground to make it easier. Only when she reached the top of the hill did she look up and when she did, she gasped at what she saw. "Ahh! Midnight! What happened to you?" Lindsay dropped her sack and ran to the corral, sliding her body through the corral cables as fast as she could. She needed to get a closer look at Midnight's tail. Midnight startled at Lindsay approaching him so quickly, and turned and trotted off. Then she could see that it was true, her eyes hadn't lied—Midnight's tail had been shredded. The tail that she spent so much time grooming, getting out every snarl. The long black tail that had nearly touched the ground was now gone. His tail was now only the length of his tailbone.

Lindsay yelled as loud as she possibly could for her voice to reach the house, "Mom! Mom! Come quick!" She examined Midnight's tail and looked around for any evidence as to what had happened. She found nothing; no hair stuck in the corral or on the ground. She wondered, *Who would want to do this and why?* Fighting off the lump in her throat, she got her saddle and bridle and tried not to think about it. His tail would grow, she knew, but she also knew that tails grow painfully slowly. She talked to Midnight as she tacked him up. "Midnight, tell me what happened? Who did this to you? How disgraceful! Don't worry, it will grow. I'll brush it everyday so it will grow fast, Okay?" Midnight's eyes gently blinked and he swished his little short tail. Once Midnight was tacked up, she walked him down to the house, "Mom! Mom!" she hollered again.

Lisa opened the door and was surprised to see that her daughter was already ready to ride, "Well, that was quick," she said walking over to help Lindsay get on her horse. "What on earth?" Lisa asked, looking at Midnight's shredded tail.

"I don't know, Mom. Something happened."

"I'll say something happened. Somebody cut Midnight's tail and they did a terrible job!"

"Who do you think did it?"

Lisa folded her arms and shouted, "Jeffrey! Beau! Come out here!" But when the boys saw Midnight's tail, Lisa could tell by the looks on their faces that they didn't do it.

"Who did that to Midnight's tail?" the boys asked, laughing.

Poor Midnight. Admittedly, he did look funny. When he swished his tail before, it looked as if he was relaxed, his long black tail taking its time, gracefully reaching around his side to shoo flies. Now, his short, shredded tail went fast, as if he was bothered: swat, swat, swat.

"Oh well, Lindsay, there's nothing we can do to change things now. You better just focus on riding Midnight right now." Lisa walked beside Lindsay and Midnight to a level spot on their property. "Go ahead and begin warming him up at a walk," Lisa said.

Lindsay was happy to do what her mother requested. "That looks good, but put your heels down a little more." Lindsay pushed her heels down as hard as she could. "That's better."

Lindsay smiled. "Are you really going to be my trainer?"

"For now, yes, and your show is only a few weeks away so I wouldn't be talking too much," Lisa said.

Lindsay giggled and said, "You sound like Anne when you say, 'Put your heels down.'"

While Lindsay warmed up Midnight, Lisa walked around and gathered objects to make jumps. Using a chair, two buckets, two logs, a hose and one smashed pipe, she contrived a jump. She propped one end of one log on the chair and the other log she propped up on the two stacked buckets, so the logs were crossed in the middle. For a ground line, she placed the smashed white plastic pipe right in front of the logs and then for extra measure, she laid the old hose down in the dirt on each side of the jump.

Lindsay continued to walk Midnight, watching to see what exactly her mother was doing. "There," Lisa said dusting her hands off. "Now I know it's not the prettiest thing you've ever seen, but I have a feeling that Midnight doesn't care if a jump is pretty or ugly."

Acting as much like a trainer as possible, Lisa directed Lindsay as she remembered Anne doing, "Okay, Lindsay, I'm pretty sure that Midnight will jump this, so go ahead and try."

Lindsay raised her eyebrows and gathered her reins. She took Midnight as far away from the jump as she could to get a running start. She steered him perfectly right in between the hoses and straight at the jump. The horse was suspicious and slowed down to look at the obstacle. Then, as if in slow motion, he jumped. In fact, he jumped straight up and too high, so Lindsay popped right out of the saddle and landed on his neck.

"Hold on, Lindsay!" Lisa yelled, running over to help her daughter who was barely hanging on. Midnight never took another step, allowing Lisa to grab her daughter and help her back in the saddle.

Lindsay's shoulders scrunched up by her ears and she began to cry. "That was scary."

"Gosh, Lindsay, it *looked* scary. What happened?"

With her teeth gritted together and a few tears dripping down her cheeks, she tried to explain, "I don't know, he just popped really high and I couldn't really hold on that good and ..."

"Okay, let's see if I can set up a better jump and maybe he'll do better next time," Lisa said encouragingly.

"I don't really want to try it again."

Lisa didn't let her end with that, and set up a smaller jump. The second time was slightly better; at least she stayed in the saddle. Again and again, Lindsay took Midnight over the little jump until they both thought it was easy. "Lindsay, I think that's enough. You've both done well."

Happy with her progress, Lindsay walked her horse back to the corral and put him away for the night.

Two weeks later when the day of the show arrived, Lindsay put a halter on a very clean and shiny Midnight and walked him confidently to the borrowed trailer in their driveway. Midnight balked at the sight of the trailer, backing up and snorting like a bull. "Midnight!" Lindsay said, as she tried again to walk him into the trailer.

Time after time, Midnight evaded entering the trailer. Time was running short, so Lisa tried to walk the horse in. He swished his body one way, then the other, doing everything he could do to keep his hooves from touching the trailer's ramp. Lisa now handed the lead rope over to Jeff, who was eager to give it a try. Midnight snorted again. Finally, just in the nick of time, Midnight reluctantly agreed to walk into the trailer.

"Yes! He's loaded!" Lindsay exclaimed.

Taking a horse to a show and being judged by judges lets a person know how they are doing. If they're training properly at home, then they should do well and get good scores. If something is going wrong with their training, then they'll score poorly. It wasn't Lindsay or Midnight's fault that day when things didn't go the way they should have. They did exactly what they'd been doing at home– popping over fences and popping out of saddles.

Once they were at the show, Lisa could see clearly that they weren't ready to be showing. During her warm up, Lindsay watched and studied the other more seasoned riders, confidently cantering their horses around and effortlessly soaring over the jumps. Just like the other riders, Lindsay headed Midnight at a jump and when Midnight jumped as boldly as Lindsay asked, it caught Lindsay off guard. Midnight flew through the air leaving Lindsay behind his motion. When they landed on the other side, Lindsay landed on Midnight's rear. Her feet had completely come out of her stirrups and her seat was no where near her saddle.

Midnight stopped dead in his tracks and waited for Lindsay to get back in the saddle. Lindsay sat for a moment in shock behind her saddle while still holding the reins and then carefully climbed back into position. Any other horse probably would have run off bucking, but not Midnight. He knew Lindsay and somehow, in his own way, tried to take care of her.

As it turned out, Lindsay and Midnight were eliminated for missing a jump on the cross-country course. It had been a long, rough day with little to be proud of, but through it all, Lindsay was proud anyway. She was proud of Midnight and that's what mattered most to Lindsay. To some, it might appear that Lindsay went home empty-handed, with no ribbon to hang on her wall. But to Lindsay, she went home with something much more special than a ribbon. For the first time, she went home with her very own horse and a smile on her face.

Chapter 9

Trail Riding

With the horse show behind them, Lisa and Lindsay enjoyed the freedom of trail riding. There were so many new sights to see and trails to explore in Windsor Heights, and mother and daughter took advantage of every opportunity they had to ride together.

There was something different about the time they spent riding than all the other time they spent together. Time seemed to not exist. Conversation was effortless. Because, somehow, mother and daughter were equals on horseback. Lindsay became seemingly bigger, stronger, and more independent, while Lisa temporarily forgot about her responsibilities and became carefree, almost childlike. Indeed, the horse was the great equalizer. For on a horse, even a small child could walk as far as an adult, trot as long or longer, run as fast or faster, and stand as tall or taller. There were no boundaries or age limits. The magic began when two things were put together—a horse … and the courage to ride.

"Can we go down to Bill's again? Midnight loves going there," Lindsay asked.

"I was really hoping we could try a different trail," her mother said.

"Let's just stop by and see if we see anybody, and then we'll go somewhere else," Lindsay asserted. Lindsay liked to see all the horses at Bill Murray's stable, and she liked to hear people that knew Midnight say hi to him.

Midnight looked good now. His winter coat had shed out revealing a sleek, glossy, jet-black summer coat, and he had gained weight. His tail was still short, but that didn't seem to matter anymore. Midnight was happy; very happy. Lindsay even said he had a happy trot.

As Lisa and Lindsay rode out of their property and onto the dirt road, Lindsay began to trot Midnight. Lisa and Moon followed, and as they approached Bill's street, Midnight automatically turned by himself. "Did you see that, Mom? Midnight knows where we're going!" Lindsay yelled.

"Yeah! I saw," Lisa yelled up to Lindsay, while trying her best to keep trotting.

They kept trotting all the way down Bill's street, and into Bill's driveway. "Mom, look at Midnight, he's doing his happy trot!" said Lindsay loudly.

Midnight had his nose stuck out ahead of him with his forelock blowing back off his forehead, and his legs were taking earth-covering strides as his hooves fell in perfect rhythm. His back was relaxed and his tail was bopping left and right.

"He is so cute!" Lisa said. Midnight was definitely happy, and Lisa and Lindsay were not the only ones to notice.

They rode right on in to the middle of Bill's place and stopped their horses. Bill Murray was

out taking care of the place when he saw them come in. He stopped what he was doing and walked over to them, "Hi, girls."

"Hi Bill," they said.

Bill looked their horses over for a moment and then asked, "Is that Midnight?"

"Yep," Lindsay said with a smile and a pat on Midnight's neck.

"Why, the way you had him trotting in here, I thought he was a Tennessee Walker. He really looks good and I like the way you have his tail," Bill said.

Lisa and Lindsay looked at each other and smirked. "Well, thank you, Bill, but we didn't really mean for it to be like that," Lisa said.

"We think Moon chewed it off," added Lindsay.

"Oh, well that's the way I like them, that's the way cowboys have to have them so they don't get too many stickers in them. I don't have any patience for brushing stickers out of long tangled tails. Well, I really need to get back to work. You girls be safe now."

"We will," Lindsay said as she proudly asked Midnight to walk on.

A lot of people were out at Bill's that day, taking care of their horses. Lisa and Lindsay were casually strolling through the stable area when a young, pretty blonde lady stepped out from behind the horse she was brushing, "Hi! Is that Midnight? Oh my gosh! It *is* Midnight!" she said, walking right up to Midnight's face. She stroked his nose and then stepped back to get a good look. "Wow! I can't believe how good he looks!" she exclaimed and then introduced herself, "Hi, I'm Launa."

"Hi, I'm Lisa and this is my daughter, Lindsay."

"Nice to meet you, my daughter and I are going out for a ride; you're welcome to come along," Launa offered enthusiastically.

"We would love to," Lisa said.

"I just need to finish saddling up my horse. It won't take but a minute."

Patience was not something that Moon had a lot of. He looked this way and that way, while Midnight stood perfectly still. Moon bobbed his head up and down, and moved his feet impatiently as Lisa tried to get him to stand still. All she wanted to do was simply stand in one place and relax a minute.

"I'm hurrying, I'm hurrying!" Launa said, noticing Moon. When she was done, she hopped on her horse, Bailey, and her daughter Megan got on behind her mother. "Have you guys been down to the Rancheros?" Launa asked.

"No, we really haven't been anywhere," said Lisa.

"Oh, well that's a really nice easy ride and it's Megan's favorite if you want to try that."

"Sure," Lindsay answered for her mother.

Now all three horses were walking down the trail and Lisa and Launa talked about how they each had three children and how they were all the same age. Launa explained how Megan doesn't like to ride by herself because she doesn't like to steer. Lindsay chatted about Midnight and how he doesn't like his baths. She asked Launa if her brown horse was a boy or a girl and how old it was. Launa said that Bailey was a mare and she was 15 years old. Megan didn't say anything except sometimes she would whisper something in her mother's ear. As they walked down Hermosa Dr., Launa pointed out some of the landmarks along the way. "Do you smell that?" Launa asked.

"Peeuu!" Lindsay exclaimed.

"What is that?" Lisa asked

Launa laughed, "I love that smell; it's onions! See that field? It's all onions. Everyone thinks it stinks, but not me. I love it." she said again, as she fanned the smell to her face.

After they passed the onion field, the smell of orange blossoms took over. "I love spring! I can never get enough of the smell of orange blossoms!" Launa exclaimed as she asked her horse to walk closer to the orange trees at the side of the road. "Hey look, the pickers missed an orange," she said plucking it from the tree. Launa rode, peeled and chatted at the same time and then offered out sections of the orange.

Megan whispered in her mother's ear. "Oh, yeah, Megan wants me to warn you about the road up ahead. We call it dead man's curve. I hate this section of road because you can't see around the corner."

Lindsay looked at her mom with her eye's wide open, "Dead man's curve?"

"As long as we stay on the right side of the road, we will be fine," assured Launa.

When they approached dead man's curve, Launa had every one stop and be still so she could listen for cars. "Okay, I don't hear anything, let's hurry up and trot around." They trotted all the way around the curve and came to a grove of Eucalyptus trees.

"This is so pretty!" Lisa said.

"Oh, I know, that's why it's our favorite trail," agreed Launa.

"Mom, haven't you always said that Eucalyptus trees are your favorite?" Lindsay asked.

"I do believe they are, Lindsay," acknowledged her mother.

Hermosa Dr. ran right through the grove of trees, breaking it up. Launa pointed, "Look, there are two trails we can take. That trail on that side of the road goes up to the hills, but this trail on this side will take us straight to the Rancheros, which is where we're going, so follow me."

As they entered the thickly wooded Eucalyptus grove, Moon snorted and seemed to get nervous. Lisa tried her best to enjoy the scenery. Midnight acted like a perfect gentleman, and Launa and Megan rode happily together on Bailey. Moon was in the back of the other horses and didn't like it. He started bobbing his head down and up and pulling on the reins. Instead of walking straight on the narrow trail like the other horses, he began prancing sideways and Lisa continued to try and get him straight.

"Maybe he would be happier in the front," Launa suggested, holding up her horse. Lisa allowed Moon to carry on his shenanigans until he reached the front of the line where he stopped dead in his tracks. He held his head high and snorted.

"Lindsay, get Midnight up here right away!" called Lisa cautiously. Lindsay immediately positioned Midnight right next to Moon which seemed to slightly comfort him. Lisa stroked Moon's neck and told him he was okay. But when she asked him to walk, he refused. Lisa kicked Moon and asked him again to walk, but he only took a step backward. "Can you walk Midnight, Lindsay?" Lindsay gently nudged Midnight and off he walked, and then Moon followed.

Lisa was embarrassed that her horse was acting up, "I'm sorry, you guys, I don't know what's wrong with him."

"How long have you had him?" Launa asked

"Not very long," Lisa replied.

"Well, I think you are very brave to ride a horse like him," Launa commented. "Is he a Thoroughbred?"

"Yes, he is and he used to race."

"I can't believe you're riding an ex-race horse, I'm too chicken to ride anything but a Quarter Horse." Launa exclaimed. "And I can't believe you're riding in an English saddle. The thought of riding in an English saddle sends chills up my spine. I like my western saddle with my good old western horn to hold on to if anything goes wrong.

Megan whispered in her mother's ear again, "How old is he?" Launa asked for her daughter.

"He's around six years old."

Launa made a grim face and said, "Oh my goodness, you are brave, I won't ride a horse any younger than ten. They just have too much spirit in them. I like my horses broke, broke, broke."

Moon settled down enough for Lisa to continue riding him through the Eucalyptus grove. The gentle, sandy trail wound around through the trees and Midnight and Lindsay led the way. It was like another world when, all at once, the trail and the trees ended. All of the horses stopped and looked at what was before them.

"Well, that's it. There's the Rancheros," Launa said in a chipper fashion.

The Rancheros was an old private riding club. There was a huge, steel-covered riding arena and a whole herd of cows in a corral right next to the arena for roping and cutting competitions. Moon snorted and sniffed in the direction of the cows.

"They usually have something going on here every night," Launa said.

"Like what?" asked Lindsay

A thoughtful expression crossed Launa's face as she recalled the events. "Monday night is barrel racing, Tuesday is team penning, Wednesday is sorting, Thursday is roping and Friday is cutting. I think."

"Hey, Mom, maybe me and Midnight can barrel race." Lindsay offered enthusiastically.

Launa began walking Bailey on in to the Rancheros and Lindsay followed on Midnight. Lisa kicked and kicked and kicked to get Moon to take a step, but he kept his big, wide-opened eyes on the cows. He seemed to not even know that he had a rider on his back. His whole body puffed up and his ears were hard forward. Step … sniff … snort, step … sniff … snort. Launa, Megan and Lindsay were watching Moon to see what he would do next. "Come on, Moon, you're fine," Lisa encouraged. Moon would only get so close to the cows and that was it, so Lisa had to get off and try to walk him up to see the cows.

Lisa tugged and tugged on his reins but to no avail. "This is ridiculous, Moon," Lisa chastised, but Moon would not budge or take his eyes off the cows.

"Mom, Midnight likes the cows!" called Lindsay.

"Yes, I can see," Lisa said unenthusiastically.

Launa turned Bailey around and walked her back by Moon to somehow comfort him. "I have to say, he is gorgeous. Scary but gorgeous," Launa said. "Why don't we start back now? If you keep riding him down here, little by little, he'll get used to the cows," she encouraged.

Lisa waved to Lindsay to bring Midnight back from visiting the cows, got back on Moon and turned him around. As they reentered the forest of Eucalyptus trees, Lindsay asked if she could canter Midnight on the soft sand.

Lisa asked Launa, "Do you guys want to canter?"

"Sure, but will he be okay?" Launa asked in regards to Moon.

"I guess we will find out," Lisa said as she gathered her reins and sunk her heels down for a firmer seat in her saddle. "Go ahead, Lindsay, you can go first."

Lindsay seemed to do nothing but think of cantering, and Midnight went off in a gentle loping fashion. Bailey went off too, with Launa and Megan enjoying their ride. Lisa gulped down her fear and gave Moon an inch of rein and off he went running, pulling for more rein. Lisa pulled back to slow the big bay horse and he went sideways on her. She gave him his reins again to straighten him out and faster he went, faster and faster until he passed Bailey and came up behind Midnight. Lisa tried to keep her seat and slow Moon down, but the more she slowed him down, the more sideways he got, and the more sideways he got, the more mad he became. Midnight glared behind him at the wild horse blowing fire from his nostrils.

The closer Moon got to Midnight, the more mad Midnight became. Midnight bucked up and kicked out at Moon. Lindsay popped out of her saddle and landed on the horn of her western saddle. Lindsay balanced and bobbled and balanced and bobbled on her stomach on the horn of the saddle while Midnight continued running to get away from Moon. "Hold on, Lindsay, don't fall!" Lisa yelled fretfully, as she herself struggled to stay on. Moon was so mad to not have his way and especially at the thought of an older horse kicking out at him that he bucked, too. All at once, seemingly in slow motion, Lindsay fell off Midnight and Lisa fell off Moon right behind her. Lisa had a hold of one rein which kept Moon from running off, but Midnight cantered off riderless through the forest of trees.

Lisa didn't care about Midnight now, she was concerned with her daughter. "Are you okay?" Lindsay was lying along the sandy trail with sticks and weeds covering her. She was crying, but tried to be strong. Lisa hugged her, and then, all at once, the sound of foot steps thundered through the trees. "Lindsay, look!" her mother pointed. Midnight was running full steam ahead, right back toward them with his reins flapping in the wind. "He's coming back for you!"

Right when it looked like the fiery, jet-black horse would trample them, he put on the brakes and stopped just inches from Lindsay. Lindsay reached out and grabbed Midnight's reins and wiped the tears from her eyes. When Launa and Megan caught back up with them, Launa looked like she had seen a ghost.

"Are you guys all right!?" Launa asked. Megan peered around from behind her mother not saying a word.

Lisa stood up, helped her daughter up and dusted her off. "I think we are fine," she said and then focused back on Lindsay, "Lindsay, are you hurt?"

Lindsay grimaced while a tear rolled down her dirty face and rubbed her stomach, "That hurt my stomach."

Launa was shaking, "Okay, that was like the scariest thing I have ever seen. You guys are crazy!" Then Launa reached in her pocket and pulled out her cell phone, "I have my cell phone, so do you want me to call for help? I can call anyone you like," she said assuredly.

"Thanks, but I think we can make it home," Lisa said, brushing Lindsay off one more time and wiping her dirty, wet face with the inside of her shirt. She then helped her back on Midnight, and spanked Moon on his neck and demanded that he be still while she got back on him.

"Okay," Launa said cautiously, "maybe we should all just walk the rest of the way home. What do you think?"

Lisa took a deep breath and dramatically blew it out, "Yeah, that would be good."

Walking back home, Moon never did mind Lisa the way she wanted him to and Launa was overly cautious at dead man's curve, making sure nothing else could possibly go wrong. Lindsay and Midnight minded their own business and plunked on ahead of the others. Launa commented again on how good Midnight looked and how she wished she would have taken him when she had the chance.

"Why didn't you take him?" wondered Lisa.

"Well, he just looked so horrible. He looked like the most miserable horse I'd ever seen, like he was just unhappy. But he doesn't look like that anymore. You guys got lucky or maybe I should say that Midnight got lucky." When they reached Bill's street, Lisa and Lindsay said goodbye to Launa and Megan. Megan didn't dare take her hands off the back of her mom's saddle to wave goodbye but she faintly whispered the words.

Once Lisa and Lindsay arrived home and after they put the horses away, Lindsay began to complain about her stomach and her side and how the saddle horn had dug deep into her stomach when she fell. Lisa told Jeff all about their trail ride, how she was concerned with Lindsay and how she didn't really like Moon. Jeff explained to Lisa again that Moon is not your average horse and what a great horse he really is. Lisa took Lindsay to the hospital that night to make sure nothing was really wrong with her, and was happy to hear the doctor say she was just bruised.

Chapter 10

Desensitizing Moon

Moon's whole life had been thought out and planned before he was ever born. His father, Al Mamoon, and mother, Hello Flo were both racehorses. And that's exactly what Moon was bred and born to be—a race horse. There was only one thing his owners expected out of him, and that was to run, very fast and *win*. Nothing more and nothing less.

It really wasn't Moon's fault then that he didn't walk kindly down the trail. It wasn't really his fault that all he wanted to do was run and not walk. He was only doing what he'd been trained to do. But now Moon had a different life, a life that did not include running fast. What Moon needed now in his new life was to be re-trained.

Lisa's new friend Launa gave her a phone number of a lady named Hillary who knew how to train horses using their natural instincts. Hillary claimed that in just a few lessons Moon would be a different horse.

Lisa was excited for Moon's first lesson. She wished Lindsay could be there but she was in school. Lisa wore her tight black riding pants with her tall black rubber boots. For a shirt, she decided on a long-sleeved, billowing, white blouse with a big draping collar and ruffles around the bottom of the extra long sleeves. It was a nice shirt for a nice occasion, not necessarily horseback-riding, but this was a special day. She brushed and curled her hair and carefully applied her make-up, thinking all the while about Moon. She brushed Moon extra heartily before tacking him up, making sure he didn't have any dirt showing to spoil his appearance.

Lisa pulled on her black leather riding gloves then carefully positioned her helmet on her head just the right way and buckled the chin strap. Lisa mounted Moon and set off for Bill Murray's stables. Moon was drowsy; he held his head low and walked quietly down the driveway. Lisa stroked the side of his neck, "You're being a very good boy, Moon," she told him calmly.

Lisa felt strange, alone on Moon walking down their dirt road in the middle of the orange groves. Everything was quiet except for the sound of Moon's hooves falling one after the other. Lisa was suspicious of Moon's laid-back attitude. Then, calmly but surely, Moon stopped walking. Lisa gently kicked his sides to cue him to continue walking. "Come on, Moon, let's go."

Moon seemed to realize that he was out alone with out Midnight to coach him through scary things, and Lisa could feel tension developing in his previously relaxed back. She stroked Moon's neck and tried her best to encourage him to not be afraid. When Moon hesitantly began walking, Lisa thought singing him a song would help keep him walking:

Half Mamoon, gentle Half Mamoon
Oh, oh what a good boy you are.
Half Mamoon, was a racehorse a long
time ago. But now you live in Riv...er...side.
Yes, Half Mamoon, Half Mamoon, people
say you won the Cal Cup, oh yes, they say
you won the Cal Cup, oh, gentle Half Mamoon.

As Lisa and Moon approached Bill's stable, Moon was fully alert, sniffing, and looking and listening in all directions. Lisa managed to make it through the stables all the way to Bill's big red barn where a short, peppy young lady was standing. She had on tight western jeans that were scrunched up at the bottom around little paddock boots, and a wad of keys dangling off her belt loop that made her look important.

"Are you Lisa?" she asked.

"Yes, I am, and you are Hillary?" confirmed Lisa while getting off Moon.

"So, this must be Moon," Hillary said as she walked around him looking at him up and down.

"Yep, this is Moon."

"He's a beautiful horse," commented Hillary, "and very smart."

"He's smart? How can you tell?"

Hillary looked at Lisa as if she were kidding, "Look at him!"

Lisa looked at him, trying to see what Hillary saw.

"Now look around at the other horses here."

Lisa looked around at the other horses standing seemingly bored in their corrals.

Hillary chuckled, "See, I told you, he's smart. You can tell by looking at him that he knows what's going on. You can't fool this one." Hillary went on in more detail, "Look at his big, clear, alert eyes, look at his ears listening to every sound, look at his nostrils flaring in and out. Yeah, he's highly alert and very smart."

Hillary stroked Moon's face and continued around him once again while stroking his neck and side. When she got around to the back side of Moon, she patted his rump and then took hold of his tail and swished it. Moon didn't seem to mind a bit having his tail swished, so she pulled on it.

Still Moon didn't mind. "So what's the problem with him?"

Lisa raised her eyebrows, "Well, for one, he spooks so much and so often on the trail that I feel as if I'm going to have a heart attack. For two, he doesn't like cows, and for three, he bucks *very high* and causes me to fall off which I don't really like. And for four, he causes wrecks on the trail."

Hillary nuzzled her nose on Moon's alert nose, totally unafraid, "Well we are going to have to fix those things then," she said to Moon. "Does he have a calm-down cue?" she asked.

"A calm-down cue?" Lisa asked perplexed. "What's that?"

Hillary explained, "Every horse should have a calm-down cue. For example, if my horse is nervous and I want him to calm down, I jiggle his right rein until he is calm. That's his calm-down cue. You should have a calm-down cue. Mine is the right rein, but it can be whatever you want it to be. Now, let me see his reins."

Lisa gladly handed Moon's reins over to Hillary, who began walking him toward the arena. Moon looked huge next to the tiny woman, who suddenly and dramatically stopped in place, spun round, looked at Moon and said, "Boo! Scared you!"

Moon copied her body language and made a dramatic stop himself. Hillary turned and continued leading him into the arena. Lisa noticed a variety of objects scattered around in the arena, an umbrella, a plastic blue tarp, a tire with a rope around it, a bag of soda cans, and some balloons. Hillary took off Moon's bridle and handed it to Lisa. "We're going to expose Moon to as much stimuli as we can to desensitize him."

Lisa quietly watched. Hillary picked up the bag of cans and jingled them in Moon's face. Moon sniffed the bag and when she put the bag down, Moon lowered his head and picked the bag up with his teeth. "You goof!" Hillary said. "Now for the umbrella, this always scares them." Hillary picked up the umbrella and proceeded to open and close it right in Moon's face but still he didn't move. When she set the opened umbrella down, Moon again picked up the umbrella with his teeth and waved it around.

Lisa and Hillary laughed. Nothing seemed to scare Moon, so she put his bridle back on and got on him. "Hand me that rope," Hillary asked Lisa, and rode Moon around and around the arena dragging the tire behind Moon with the rope. "That's weird, nothing seems to bother him," Hillary commented.

Just when Lisa thought Hillary was finished, she said, "Let's see how he moves."

"What do you mean?" wondered Lisa.

Hillary took Moon over to a round pen and took off his bridle once again and his saddle. Hillary stood in the middle of the round pen and shooed Moon off into a run. Moon ran and ran and then Hillary jumped in front of him causing him to change his direction and run the other way. Hillary squatted down and studied the big Thoroughbred as he continued running, "He's awesome!"

"He is?" Lisa asked, surprised.

"He moves great and he is so well-proportioned and balanced. How much did you pay for him?"

"Five hundred."

"Well, He's worth five times that, right this minute."

"He is?"

"Where did you get him?"

"From a lady who got him off the racetrack."

"Whoa, whoa," Hillary said in a soothing tone of voice to Moon who proceeded to stop. Hillary stayed in a squatting position and turned her back to Moon. Hillary talked to Lisa with out even looking at Moon, "He should be licking his lips right now."

Lisa nodded.

"Is he dropping his head?" Hillary asked, and Lisa nodded again. "Now I am waiting for him to walk up to me submissively."

Lisa nodded as Moon gently walked over to Hillary with his head held low. He sniffed her hair and she stood up and praised him. "Good boy." She explained to Lisa, "He trusts me now. You have to build your trust with horses." Hillary stroked Moon's face, neck and sides again but this time, when she got to his back side, she paused, patted his rump and then hugged him from behind by wrapping her arms around his back legs.

"Isn't that dangerous?" Lisa exclaimed.

"Only if you don't trust your horse, but I trust him. And because I trust him, he wants to trust me. So, you said he raced? Did he win?"

Lisa smiled, "They said he won the California Cup Mile, but I don't really know if it's true."

"Does he have a tattoo?"

Lisa looked bewildered, "A tattoo? Um, no, I haven't seen a tattoo on him."

"Have you looked under his lip?"

"No."

Hillary lifted Moon's upper lip, "Yep, he's got one. Look."

Lisa held Moon's lip just the way Hillary did and there to her surprise was a number tattooed on the inside, delicate, pink skin of Moon's lip.

Hillary advised Lisa, "It's easier to read in the dark with a flash light, so tonight, when it's dark, have someone hold a flash light on it and you still might be able to read it before it fades any more. If you can read the number, then you can

call the Jockey Club and get all of his information' including any races he might have won."

Lisa was excited that she could now find out the truth about Moon. She thanked Hillary for the lesson and started home. Slightly suspicious of Moon's rather reasonable attitude, she decided to be on the safe side and sing Moon another song. She sang and sang until they were both safely home.

That very night, Jeff helped Lisa read the number off Moon's lip. It was no easy task because when Jeff would flip his lip up and hold the flashlight on the tattoo, and Lisa wrote down the numbers, Moon would pull his head away, so they would have to start all over again. The tattoo was faded and hard to read, but finally, Lisa had a number and hoped it was the right one. The next day, she called the Jockey Club and gave the lady the tattoo number and requested his records. The lady said that the tattoo number belonged to a bay gelding named Half MaMoon.

"Can you tell me if he won the Cal Cup?" requested Lisa.

"Mam, all I can tell with my records is that he raced in the 1997 Cal Cup, I can't tell you what place he came in, but you can order a video of that race if you want," offered the operator.

Lisa ordered the tape and two weeks later a box arrived in the mail. It was Moon's video. That night after dinner, the whole family sat down and played the video. Lindsay, Jeffrey and Beau sat attentively as the tape began to play.

As the video played, one racehorse and jockey after another were led out onto the track by a pony horse. The pony horse and rider were there to comfort the high-strung racehorses and jockeys, making sure that nothing happened to either one of them in all the excitement before the race began. The pony horses were well behaved, stout Quarter Horses. They wore western saddles and over their necks they had a big piece of leather that prevented the nervous racehorses from biting their necks. The pony horse riders were calm, riding with just one hand so they could hold the reins of the racehorse they were leading. The jockeys wore bright-colored silks with helmets and goggles, and the horses were sleek and slender like racecars. The announcer called the names of each horse and jockey as they walked by:

"#1 is *Skywalker's Choice,* ridden by Corey Nakatani.

#2 is *Canyon Crest,* ridden by Julio Garcia.

#3 is *Play It By Ear,* ridden by Corey Black.

#4 is *Hoe Down Be Good*, ridden by David Nuesch.

#5 is *Half Mamoon*, ridden by Gary Stevens."

Lisa's heart skipped a beat when she saw Moon. "There he is!"

"Yep, there he is," Jeff said proudly.

"#6 is *Arrivederci Baby*, ridden by Miguel Perez.

#7 is *Uronurown*, ridden by C. Hummel.

#8 is *Bat Eclat*, ridden by David Flores.

#9 is *Gastown*, ridden by Alex Solis

#10 is *Patriotaki*, ridden by Martin Pedroza."

Once all the horses were led out on to the track, they were escorted one-by-one into the starting gate. Some horses were afraid to enter the gate and had to be shoved in from behind by three or four men. Moon looked afraid and balked a little but walked in anyway and they shut the gate behind him. As soon as all the horses were locked in their own start gate, all the gates flew open at the same time and the horses exploded onto the track. The announcer with his English accent immediately began calling the race exactly as he saw it in a steady stream of words, drawing a breath only when he was absolutely out of air:

"Here for the Early Times California Cup Mile, they are sent on their way to a good beginning, it's *Hoedown B. Good* going straight to the lead with *Play It By Ear* getting up second and *Arrivederci Baby* in the blue colors, *Gastown* on the extreme outside. (breath) *Skywalker's Choice* is taken back down at the rail to race just off the leaders, *Bat Eclat* up along side of him and *Uronurown* in the pink colors moving up there as well. (breath) Then we come back to *Half Mamoon* 3rd last and six lengths off those leaders, *Patriotaki* 2nd last and *Canyon Crest* brings up the rear. (breath)"

Lisa, Jeff, Lindsay, Jeffrey and Beau sat wide-eyed watching the race. "They lied, there's no way Moon won this race," Lisa said.

"Quiet!" Jeff said again.

"They've run to the ¾ pole and *Play It By Ear* has taken a hold of the bit and he's quickened the pace, now they weren't going that fast earlier but *Play It By Ear* is sprinting away from them now. (breath) In second place is *Hoe Down Be Good* and then *Arrivederci Baby*, *Gastown* on the outside and *Uronurown* in the red colors down at the rail. (breath) *Skywalker's choice* is 6th, five lengths off the leaders followed by *Bat Eclat* and then we come back to *Half MaMoon* whose got seven lengths to make up. (breath)"

"*Seven* lengths to make up?" Lisa shook her head in disappointment.

"Shhh!" said Jeff.

"Another four back to *Canyon Crest* and *Patriotaki*. (breath) They run the 3/8 and *Play it By Ear, Hoe Down B. Good* comes right back at him at the rail, and *Hoe Down Be Good* takes a slight lead, *Uronurown* in with a shot in third.

(breath) On the outside, *Arrivederci Baby*, then *Gastown*, *Skywalker's Choice* along side of him and *Half Mamoon* is starting a run on the extreme outside, then *Bat Eclat*. (breath)"

Jeff looked at Lisa with a spark in his eye and a slight smile starting out of the corner of his mouth, "Moon's picking it up!"

"Top of the lane at the rail *Hoe Down Be Good*, *Play It By Ear* coming right back at him, *Gastown*, *Half MaMoon* on the grand stand side is coming *flying*! (breath)"

Jeff scooted to the edge of his seat with his eyes glued to the television, Lisa's jaw dropped and the kid's began cheering for Moon, "Come on, Moon, faster, you can do it!" they yelled.

"*Half Mamoon* in the green on the extreme outside, *mowing* them all down! *Gastown* chasing him home. (breath)"

Lisa jumped up off the couch and shouted, "Go, Moon! Go!"

"*Half Mamoon, Gastown, Half Mamoon* has *won* the Cal Cup Mile! *Gastown* second, *Patriotaki* gets up for third."

"Wow, I can't believe he actually won! I thought he would lose for sure!" Lisa exclaimed. "He was so far behind."

Jeff, now the proud owner of *Half Mamoon* had a smile from ear to ear, "I knew he was a champion! I told you he was great!"

"Moon ran fast, huh, Mom?" Beau chimed in.

"Can we watch it again?" asked Jeffrey.

"We sure can, son!" said Jeff as he rewound the tape and pressed PLAY again.

They cheered for Moon the second time as well, making sure he won again.

After the second time watching the race, Lisa commented, "Gosh, I almost didn't think he would win again even though I knew he would."

"Mom, did you see Moon's ears when he crossed the finish line? They shot up like parachutes!" Lindsay said with a giggle. Lindsay pressed REWIND and PLAY and REWIND and PLAY several times watching Moon's ears go from laying back as he raced to the finish to popping forward like parachutes to slow him down once he crossed the finish line.

Now Jeff stood up and proclaimed proudly, "I'm going up the hill to see my horse. I think he could use a carrot about now."

Everyone else jumped up, also wanting to go too.

All the way up the hill, Jeff assured himself of what a fine champion of a horse Moon was. "Hey, Moon!" Jeff called.

Moon walked over to see what the whole family wanted. "We brought you a carrot." Jeff roughly petted Moon's neck and scratched under his chin. "Yeah, you are a good boy. You're a champ, aren't ya! And the Cal Cup Winner."

Moon was a champion after all; he proved that the day he won the Cal Cup Mile. Moon had clearly fulfilled the purpose for which he was born—to win races. He had other victories to his name, but none compared to the way he ran in the Cal Cup. The way he came from the back, swept around the outside and passed the whole field of horses with room to spare at the finish line showed his courage and sheer determination. How proud his owners must have been of him that

day, cheering for him, taking pictures with him in the winner's circle with the famous jockey Gary Stevens who rode Moon to victory.

But who stood around him the day he raced so hard that he bowed his tendon and couldn't race anymore? Who cheered for him at that very moment, when his life as a racehorse was over. What could he do now? He'd been born to race, not be a family horse. Could his courage and determination pull him through to a new beginning with a new life and family? The Wrights hoped Moon could become the horse they needed, a horse for Lisa and eventually a horse for Lindsay.

Chapter 11

A Historical Swim

It was summertime, and the days were long and hot. Lindsay, Jeffrey, and Beau were out of school now, and the mornings were lazy. But not this morning, "I want you guys to get dressed right away today. I have something planned," Lisa said to the children who were wandering out of their rooms in their pajamas.

"What are we going to do?" Lindsay asked.

"I think it's a great day to go on a walk with Cheyenne and Sugar. But I don't want to wait too long or it will be too hot," answered her mother.

Jeffrey overheard 'walk' and didn't like the idea of it. "Do we have to go?"

"Jeffrey, look outside," Lisa said, pointing out their big picture window off in the distance to the walkers and bikers on the canal.

"Can I at least ride my bike?"

"Can I ride Midnight?" Lindsay quickly blurted out.

"Let's just start with getting dressed and having breakfast and then we will decide."

During breakfast, Jeff chatted with the kids before leaving for work. Lisa told him their plan of going on a walk and taking the dogs. "Why are you taking the dogs?"

"Honey, everyone walks their dogs on the canal; I thought it would be fun."

"Well, make sure they wear their collars and leashes," Jeff said as he gave Lisa a kiss goodbye. "I love you, be careful, okay?"

It was finally decided that Jeffrey and Beau would ride their bikes, Lindsay would walk Cheyenne, and Lisa would walk Sugar. The dogs were happy to be out on their leashes, and held their heads high as they walked down the long, long driveway. They crossed the dirt road and then a field before coming to the canal.

The Gage Canal was over 100 years old and was the main water source for the acres and acres of orange groves in Windsor Heights. It was about 6 feet wide and 4 feet deep, with a dirt road on each side of it. The water level varied, but today it was high. The rippling water looked refreshing as it passed along the historic canal. As they walked along the road on one side of the canal, an occasional jogger or biker would pass by on the other side. Sugar stopped and crawled to the edge of the canal to get a drink. She lapped a little water, then walked a little. She seemed to have a smile on her face as she went back for another drink. "Sugar wants to get in the canal, I think," said Lisa.

"Hey, look," called Lindsay, "Cheyenne is copying Sugar!" Cheyenne edged herself carefully to the canal's edge to ever so slightly wet her tongue. Cheyenne wouldn't dare get in the canal, for she hated water.

"Mom, where exactly are we going?" Jeffrey wondered, wiping a single drop of sweat from his brow.

"Jeffrey, don't worry about it, what matters is that we're having a great time."

Jeffrey took a deep breath and began pedaling again. Lisa called up to Jeffrey to give him a better answer, "Actually, Jeffrey, I thought you and Beau might like to see the Rancheros."

"Yeah, Jeffrey, you and Beau can see the cows down there," Lindsay said encouragingly.

The Rancheros was a short horseback ride, but a very long walk on foot. Lisa was confident the children and the dogs could make it. They cut through some orange groves to shorten the distance, but in the aisles of trees were sticks and trenches for water which made it impossible for the boys to ride their bikes. Jeffrey and Beau were now pushing their bikes through the groves when suddenly little Beau could take it no longer. He stopped pushing his bike and looked up at his mother in the middle of the forest of orange trees and asked, "Are you sure this is the way to Aunt Carrows?"

Lisa laughed, but felt bad that she had led the kids on what seemed to be a wild goose chase. "Beau," Lisa said, hugging her five-year-old, "I said we were going to the Rancheros, not Aunt Carrows."

"Beau, we don't even have an Aunt Carrow," Lindsay clarified.

"Can we please go back now?" begged Jeffrey.

"I guess, maybe it's best if we start home now," Lisa offered.

Lisa let Beau walk Cheyenne as she pushed his bike back through the grove and back onto the canal. When they emerged onto the canal, there wasn't a person in sight. Lisa couldn't resist the urge to let the dogs off their leashes just for a minute, and called to Lindsay, "Let Sugar off her leash." Lindsay looked at her mother with concern. "Go ahead Linds, just for a couple of minutes to let them run around."

"Okay, what ever you say," Lindsay said smartly.

Lisa then unhooked Cheyenne's leash and they all continued toward home on the canal road. The sun shone down strong and hot and the water looked so refreshing. Sugar couldn't seem to resist the call of the fresh water as she continued making frequent stops for drinks.

Suddenly out of nowhere, a man appeared on the opposite side of the canal walking a big dog. Cheyenne immediately showed her disapproval by barking as if she owned the place. She ran after the dog, and was so focused on it on the other side of the canal that she didn't notice the water ... and accidentally ran straight into the canal. Her whole body became submerged except her long velvet ears which floated on top of the water.

The kids laughed and laughed as Cheyenne quickly changed her mind about the big dog and swam to the edge of the canal. Lisa bent over and pulled her out by the nape of her neck to safety. "What on earth were you thinking, Cheyenne?"

Cheyenne wagged her tail and shook off the awful water. Sugar could stand it no longer. This time when she bent down to get a drink, she purposely, and slowly slipped her big body down into the water. As Sugar floated down stream, she smoothly paddled her legs to swim. Sugar was so big that she gently rolled to one side, then to the other as she kept afloat.

Finally, she swam to the edge and tried to get out. She tried and tried but couldn't pull herself out. Lisa and Lindsay both grabbed hold of Sugar's collar and pulled the happy dog out. Sugar romped around in the dirt and then jumped back in the canal to do it all over again. She floated and rolled, and floated and rolled, just like before and then asked to get out again.

Lisa put the dirty, wet dogs back on their leashes and they continued their trek home. As the Riverside

sun beat down, the children began to complain.

"I'm hot," Beau said.

"I'm thirsty," added Jeffrey.

"Can we swim when we get home?" Lindsay begged.

When they were almost home, near the Adam's Street bridge, Lisa had an idea, "You guys are hot, right?"

"Yeah," they chorused.

"Okay, then, take off your shoes and socks."

When the children looked perplexed, Lisa said, "Trust me, just take them off."

The children sat down in the dirt and proceeded to follow their mother's instructions.

"Okay, now go swimming," Lisa said pointing to the canal.

"What?" Lindsay shrieked dramatically.

"You heard me, go swimming. The water's great and shallow enough to stand up."

Jeffrey cautiously shook his head, "Oh, no."

"You guys, come on, listen," Lisa started, "A long, long, time ago when Riverside was first founded, this is where everyone came to swim. There were no pools back then, I even read about children actually learning to swim in the Gage Canal. Sugar liked it, didn't she?" The children listened and then with faint, coy smiles, they cautiously walked to the canal's edge to get a good look.

"I'll put my feet in, but that's it," Lindsay asserted. The boys agreed with their sister.

All three children sat down and dangled their bare feet in the cool water.

Lisa was happy for them but still she pressed, "Look, you guys will have a lot more fun if you just jump in. You can float downstream a little ways and then get out. It'll be great."

Lindsay took a hard look at the bottom of the

canal, "Mom, do you know how much moss is on the bottom of the canal? I'm not touching that!"

"Okay, then, put on your socks and you won't feel it."

Lindsay thought for a second and then said, "Okay, then I will." Lindsay pulled her socks on over her wet feet, which were coated with a layer of dirt. She then walked back to the canal's edge and dangled her feet in the water again. "I'm not so sure about this, it's gross."

"Lindsay, I promise, it's going to be fun. You can float and hold your feet up," encouraged Lisa.

"Well, if *you* think it looks like so much fun, then *you* go in," Lindsay smarted.

The boys watched and waited to see what would happen next. "Lindsay, I have to hold the dogs. Look, just jump in and try it. If you don't like it, then get out."

Lindsay quieted down as she stared down at the water, evaluating the green, slimy moss waving around at the bottom of the canal. "Well, I am hot and I do have my socks on." Without another word, Lindsay pushed her body off the edge and into the canal. "Whew, it's cool," she said, with her breath half taken away. "Come on, Jeffrey, get in, come on, Beau." The boys looked at one another and seemingly agreed together to get in with their sister. Soon all three children were standing in the canal.

"Lie on your backs and float now," instructed their mother.

The kids laughed as they each tried to float. "Oooo, moss touched my toes!" Jeffrey said with a bad look on his face.

"You should have put your socks on, Jeffrey. I can't feel it." Lindsay said proudly.

Little Beau's jaw began to chatter with joy as he frolicked in the shallow water. "Beau, do you want to get out?" Lisa asked. Beau shook his head no. Lisa laughed and smiled as she watched the children play the way the children of long ago played when suddenly a car honked. It was Jeff in his truck, crossing the Adams Street bridge! He motioned for Lisa to come over to his truck. "Hi, honey," Lisa started.

"What are the kids doing in the canal?" Jeff asked sternly.

"Er ... they're cooling off," Lisa replied cautiously.

"Get them out of there!" he quickly demanded.

"Honey, don't be upset. This is where the children from long ago learned how to swim, it was totally normal back then."

Jeff shook his head at Lisa's reasoning, "Don't give me that 'children from long ago' nonsense. The children from long ago also didn't have a clean pool to swim in. I might as well go home and fill our pool in with dirt, and you guys can just swim in the canal from now on!"

"Fine, don't worry; I'm getting them out right now."

Jeff shook his head again and said, "I just can't believe you let the kids swim in the canal!" He stared for a moment in disbelief at the children frolicking and floating in the canal and added, "No, actually I can believe it!" And then he drove off.

One by one, Lisa helped the kids get out of the canal and onto the dirt road. They slipped their shoes on and dripped dry all the way home. Lisa didn't want Jeff to be upset, but she couldn't help but be glad that the kids had had a chance to play like the children of long ago—wet, dirty, and happy.

Chapter 12

Penny and Her Palomino

One summer day in the middle of July, Lisa and Lindsay woke up extra early to feed Moon and Midnight. If they fed early, then they could ride early, before the boys woke up.

Lindsay tossed both Moon and Midnight a big, green flake of sweet alfalfa hay.

As the horses munched on their breakfast, Lisa brushed their coats and picked out their feet so right when they were done eating, they would be ready for their saddles and bridles.

Soon, mother and daughter were plunking down the road side-by-side. Lisa asked Lindsay,

"Don't you think it would be fun if the boys rode with us?"

"Yeah, but we only have two horses," Lindsay clarified. "Mom, can we please stop by Bill's first today?"

"I guess it wouldn't hurt anything."

There was a special feeling in the warm air that morning. The palm trees on St. Lawrence gently fluttered in the sky high above as both horses quietly walked on. "Moon's being a really

good boy, isn't he?" Lisa asked, eager to hear her daughter agree.

"Actually," Lindsay started raising her eyebrows, "he is."

As Moon and Midnight automatically turned into Murray's Ranch, Lisa and Lindsay noticed a girl in Bill's field, sitting on a beautiful big, golden Palomino. She was riding in a western saddle with a fancy western breast collar, complete with a western style bridle. Lisa and Lindsay looked at one another and without saying a word, walked directly toward the girl. The big Palomino stood square, unafraid of the strange horses approaching. As soon as Lindsay was close enough for the girl to hear her, she called, "I like your horse, what's its name?"

"Her name's Bunny. Are you guys going out on the trail?"

"Yeah, we are. Do you want to go with us?" Lisa offered.

"Sure. I'm so tired of riding alone."

"What's your name?" Lindsay asked.

"Penny. What's yours?"

"I'm Lindsay, and this is Midnight," Lindsay stated proudly.

"I'm Lisa, Lindsay's mom, and this is my horse Moon."

"Oh, you're lucky your mom rides with you," Penny commented. "And you're lucky you guys get to ride Thoroughbreds! I wish my parents would buy me a Thoroughbred. I'm only allowed to ride Quarter Horses."

Lisa smiled at the young girl, "Are you kidding? I can't believe you are riding a Palomino! Do you know how long I have dreamt of having a Palomino?"

"Midnight is half Quarter Horse and half Thoroughbred," clarified Lindsay.

Moon could take no more small talk, and began bobbing his head up and down, impatiently. "Moon, relax," requested Lisa trying to cue him with his right rein to calm him down. "Come on, you guys, let's start walking."

As the three horses began walking, Lisa admired Penny. She seemed so young, but so mature to be out on the trail by herself. She looked so capable on her western Palomino, in her western saddle, and her western split reins. She looked like she took good care of her horse. All four of Bunny's legs were wrapped up with red protective wraps, and her red saddle pad matched perfectly. Penny sat straight up in the saddle with her shoulders held slightly back, and her dark, curly hair was in sharp contrast to her horse's golden coat.

"Do you guys want to go to my favorite field to canter?" Penny suggested.

"Sure!" Lindsay agreed.

Penny's favorite field was a softly plowed field, right next to the canal. As soon as they set foot on the field, Penny politely asked, "Do you mind if I canter?"

"Go ahead," Lisa said.

Penny took her split reins one in each hand and held them down at her thighs. Bunny tucked her head and gently loped along, full of beauty, while Penny comfortably rocked back and forth in her western saddle.

She came to a stop along side of Lisa and Moon, "Your turn!"

"Yeah, Mom, your turn," encouraged Lindsay.

"Okay, I guess I'll try." Lisa gathered her reins, adjusted her seat in her saddle, and hoped for the best. "Come on, Moon, giddy up!" Moon was agreeable and cantered through the field with his long Thoroughbred stride. Lisa tried to imitate Penny, the way she sat so nicely in the saddle.

Penny shouted across the field, "That looks so cool!"

Just like Penny, Lisa cantered right up along side of Penny and Lindsay, and came to a stop.

Penny stared at Moon, "He is so beautiful! You guys look so awesome together!"

Lisa smiled, "We do?"

Penny looked at Lindsay, "They looked awesome, didn't they?"

"Yeah, Mom, that did look good."

"Your turn," Penny said in a chipper fashion looking at Lindsay.

Lindsay gladly asked Midnight to do just as Bunny and Moon had done. Midnight obeyed Lindsay's every cue, and Lindsay couldn't have been more proud.

"You guys are lucky you get to ride in English saddles. I've been wanting an English saddle for so long," Penny said desperately.

At this point, Lindsay felt bad for Penny and had an idea, "Do you want to try Midnight?"

"I thought you'd never ask," Penny said, jumping down from her horse. Lindsay slowly lowered herself down from Midnight and the girls switched reins. Lindsay and Penny looked eye to eye and Penny asked, "How old are you?"

"I'll be ten in a few weeks."

"No fair! You're as tall as me!"

Now that they were on the subject of age, Lisa asked Penny how old she was.

"I'm twelve and a half. I know, I'm short. I'm just hoping to be at least five feet tall. I don't think I can bear the thought of saying 'Four-feet-eleven' for the rest of my life."

Lisa chuckled at Penny's drama. Penny instructed Lindsay on just how to hold the reins so Bunny would hold her head nice. Lindsay split the reins and held them on her thighs just as Penny did. Likewise, Lindsay told Penny how to hold Midnight's English reins with her pinkies properly tucked out of her grip.

"Let's go together, okay?" Penny offered.

"Okay," Lindsay said willingly.

Lindsay and Penny cantered around the soft field side-by-side, leaving a cloud of dust behind them. Moon didn't like being left behind, so Lisa let Moon take her for a ride through the dust to catch up with Bunny and Midnight. Lisa was glad when they all came to a stop so she could catch her breath and get the dirt out of her eyes. Lindsay was beaming, "Mom, that was so fun, Bunny is so smooth, you have to try her!"

Penny agreed, "Go ahead, anyone can ride Bunny. Do you mind if I try Moon?"

"No, not at all, but are you allowed to? What about your Mom and Dad?" Lisa asked.

"They won't mind, as long as I'm with an adult."

"Well, would you mind wearing my helmet? Lisa asked, taking it off and offering it to Penny.

Penny took the helmet and buckled it under her chin. She then tried to get on Moon but couldn't get her short, little leg high enough to get it in the stirrup iron. Penny turned around and smiled a coy smile, "A little help, please?" she asked with one leg lifted off the ground signaling for a leg up. Lisa got behind Penny and grabbed her ankle and hoisted the young girl up on Moon. "Whoa, he's tall!"

"Be careful," insisted Lisa.

"Oh, I will. Besides, I take lessons."

Lisa easily slipped her foot in the stirrup of Penny's western saddle and gently straddled the stout Palomino. She took a moment to admire the beauty of a horse with a golden coat and ran her fingers through Bunny's white mane. "This is amazing! I can't believe I am finally on a Palomino!"

Penny cantered Moon in big circles around Midnight and Bunny. "You're so lucky, I love this horse!" she called as she continued cantering.

"He's showing off for Bunny, Mom," Lindsay noticed.

"You're right. That's probably why he's being good."

Penny rode Moon brilliantly and brought him to a stop in front of Bunny. "Okay, it's your turn to try Bunny," Penny offered to Lisa.

Lisa asked the well-trained Quarter Horse for

a slow lope and that's exactly what Bunny gave her. Smoothly, like a rocking chair Bunny went, not pulling on the reins, not threatening to buck, just doing only what she was asked. Lisa smiled, and stopped her right in front of Moon and Midnight. "Wow, that was great! She's really well-trained." Moon was happy to have Bunny standing right in front of him, but Midnight pinned his ears at her, and snarled, showing his teeth.

"Midnight!" Lindsay reprimanded. "Don't you do that to Bunny."

"Bunny has had years and years of professional training. My dad said that the only way he would allow me to ride out on the trails was if I was on a well-trained Quarter Horse. So I guess I can't complain, I just think Thoroughbreds are so much more fun and especially riding them in an English saddle. I'm going to beg my Mom for an English saddle as soon as I get home!"

Riding home, Lindsay was entertained just listening to Penny go on and on about how she loved English. "How many horses do you have?" Lindsay asked.

"Three. Bunny, Mighty Mouse and Bunny's baby who is in training."

Lindsay dropped her jaw, "You have a baby in training?"

"Yeah, but we won't get her back for almost a year. My dad insists on a well-trained horse."

Lisa was curious. "Who's Mighty Mouse?"

"Oh, he's our old pony. I think he's almost thirty, or something ancient like that, but we still ride him."

"Are you allowed to let anyone else ride him? Lindsay has two younger brothers, and I was thinking …"

Penny knew what Lisa was thinking, "My mom would definitely let your boys ride him, but I would have to be there because, well, he's kind of weird."

"What do you mean by weird?"

"Mighty Mouse is a Hackney Pony and he has, like, this really high knee action. He used to pull carts but I wanted to ride him so I broke him to ride when no one was looking. My mom was so mad at me but she doesn't care now because he's so old."

"Would you by chance have an extra saddle?"

"Don't even worry about that, we have so many saddles. I don't want to brag or anything, but my dad is a lawyer, so yeah, we have a lot of saddles."

Lisa smiled at Penny's innocence.

Once they got back to Murray's Ranch, Penny didn't want to go her separate way so she continued on with Lisa and Lindsay all the way back to their house. "Now that I know where you live, maybe we can ride together sometimes. It's an easy trail ride to get here, it would probably only take me ten to fifteen minutes."

Lisa got Penny's phone number, and said they would call her to go riding another day.

Lindsay couldn't help herself, "My birthday's coming up. Maybe you can come over then."

"I'd love to! Well, I guess I better get Bun Bun home," Penny said patting Bunny's rump. She turned her big Palomino around and headed towards home. Bunny walked off in a most agreeable fashion, safe as stitches.

Meanwhile, Moon whinnied pathetically at the sight of a beautiful Palomino mare leaving him.

He tossed his head disagreeably when Lisa made him walk back to his corral. Lindsay let Midnight canter one last time up to the top of the hill.

After Moon and Midnight were put away, mother and daughter walked back down the hill to the house. They were relaxed, dirty, and satisfied. They chatted about Penny and her Palomino and Lindsay's upcoming birthday and then, just as Lindsay opened the door to the house to go in, Lisa exclaimed sharply. "Lindsay! Look at your boots, they're filthy! You weren't planning on going in the house with those on, were you?"

Lindsay stopped dead in her tracks and looked down at her feet, "Umm, no?" She turned around and sat down on the porch step, "Can you help me pull them off?"

As her mother went to pull off her boots, Lindsay smiled thoughtfully.

"What are you smiling about?"

Lindsay explained, "It's just kind of weird because when we ride, it's kind of like you're my friend, but then when we get home, you turn back into my mom."

Lisa smiled that Lindsay had caught on to what she herself had known all along.

Chapter 13

Stop That Pony!

'Ding dong,' the door bell sounded, setting Sugar and Cheyenne off like sirens. The more Cheyenne barked, the more Sugar barked.

Jeffrey and Beau raced through the house to see who was ringing the bell. The glass window panes in the front door made it easy to see the visitor.

"Mom, there's a girl here," Jeffrey called in his usual calm fashion as he opened the door.

Lindsay ran to see exactly who was there. "Mom, Penny's here!"

"Hi, Lindsay," said Penny. "I'm sorry I didn't call or anything, because like, I didn't know your number, but I brought Mighty Mouse over."

"You did?" said Lindsay and then quickly introduced Penny to her two younger brothers.

"Do you and your brothers want to ride?" Penny asked.

Before answering, Lindsay, Jeffrey, and Beau stepped out on the front porch to see the horses Penny had brought over. Bunny and Mighty Mouse were tied to a small fence in the front of the house.

Might Mouse was a grayish, brownish, slender-looking pony. Penny had the pony fully prepared for a possible ride, complete with a child-sized western saddle. Although he was 30 years old, he didn't seem old. "So do you guys want to ride?"

Jeffrey and Beau looked at one another and smiled. Lisa had finally made her way out of the house to see what all the commotion was about. "Oh hi, Penny. So that's Mighty Mouse," Lisa said knowingly.

"Yep, I was hoping we could all go riding," Penny said.

"That's really nice that you brought him over all ready to ride," Lisa said and then asked the boys, "Do you guys want to ride?" Jeffrey and Beau nodded.

Penny beamed with excitement and discussed her plan, "Okay, this is what I was thinking: Lindsay, you can ride Bunny and Jeffrey can ride Midnight. Your little brother Beau can ride Mighty Mouse and I'll ride Moon."

"Cool, I get to ride Bunny," Lindsay aired.

Lisa chimed in, "I guess it looks like I'm not riding."

Penny quickly rethought her plan, "Oh, I'm sorry, Lindsay and I can ride double on Bun Bun and you can ride Moon."

"No, that's okay. If you want to ride Moon, then I want you to ride him. I'm sure Jeffrey will be fine on Midnight and Lindsay will be fine on Bunny, but I'm not so sure about Beau and Mighty Mouse," Lisa said cautiously.

"Don't even worry about it, I can hook Mighty

up to a lead rope and pony Beau. Trust me, nothing will happen."

Lindsay and the boys ran back into the house to get ready for their first ride. Jeffrey wasn't exactly excited, but since there was nothing better to do, he willingly went along with the idea. Little Beau followed Lindsay around and waited to be pointed in the right direction.

"Beau, you need to get on some long pants, okay?" Lindsay directed.

Beau ran to his room, yanked his jeans from his closet, and ran them back to his big sister to get her approval, "Lindsay, can I wear these?"

"Yes, now hurry and put them on."

Penny made good use of her time and tacked up Moon and Midnight, leading them both down the hill to the house. Soon, everyone was holding a horse and ready to mount. Penny held up her lower leg and gave Lisa the same pleading look she had seen before, "Do you mind?" she asked.

Lisa grabbed Penny's ankle and hoisted the girl up on Moon and then helped Jeffrey on Midnight. Jeffrey was stout and heavy, and seemed out of place on a horse. His right ankle was still weak from breaking his leg, and turned in toward the horse. "Jeffrey, sit up straight and point both of your toes straight ahead," directed Lisa.

Jeffrey tried, but couldn't manage to find the strength in that one ankle to turn it straight. Ignoring Jeffrey's ankle issues, Lisa turned her attention to Beau. "Upsidaisy, Beau," she said, picking him up and sitting him squarely in the small saddle on Mighty Mouse. Lindsay was the only one who got on her horse without any help.

Mighty Mouse got a spark in his eyes and looked straight as an arrow down the driveway. He chomped on his bit and held his head high. Beau said not a word as he tried to settle on the strange pony. "Penny, are you sure he's good on the trail?" Lisa asked, with concern in her voice.

"He really is, but he probably just wants to go home right now."

"Beau, hold the reins like this and if you want to stop, just pull back like this. If you want to go this way, then hold the reins over here and if you want to go that way, then hold the reins here," demonstrated his mother. "I am going to get your helmet out of the garage so don't do anything and don't kick him, okay? Just wait right here and don't move."

As soon as Lisa was just a few feet away from the pony, the pony made a break for it, picking up its knees and high-stepping it down the driveway. "Beau, hold on!" Lisa yelled, running after him barefoot.

Beau held on to the saddle horn, and bounced up and down out of the saddle seat all the way down the driveway. Lisa ran as fast as she could, but couldn't catch that high stepping pony. Luckily, there were some grove workers along side of the orange grove, so she yelled, "Help! Stop that pony!"

It did no good, because all the workers managed to do was stare at the frantic barefoot mother chasing after a high-stepping pony. Still Lisa ran, because there was no telling what might happen if Mighty Mouse made it to the end of the driveway and out onto the road. Just when Lisa thought the worst, Lindsay came running up from

behind her on the big, stout Palomino. Lindsay ran Bunny down the side of the orange grove and cut Mighty Mouse off at the end of the driveway.

"Oh, no you don't, Mighty Mouse," Lindsay said, bending down over Bunny's neck and grabbing the pony's reins.

Lisa stepped into a shady spot on the hot asphalt to cool her feet and catch her breath, as Lindsay led Beau and Mighty Mouse back up the driveway to get his helmet. Lisa walked gingerly on her aching feet back up to the house. Once she was within earshot of Penny, Penny apologized, "I'm so sorry, I had no idea he would run off. I was going to catch him, but I didn't want to run after him on Moon, because I thought I'd scare Mighty Mouse even more. So that's why Lindsay got him with Bunny."

Lisa was still breathing hard, "I knew he looked like a spirited pony, even if he is old."

"If you have a lead rope, I can attach it to his bridle and I guarantee he won't get away. But Lindsay will have to hold it because she's on Bunny," Penny explained.

Lisa wiped away the tears from Beau's cheeks and put on his helmet. Beau didn't want to go anymore, but his mother encouraged him to try once more, and promised him nothing would happen.

Finally, with Mighty Mouse properly secured, all four kids headed out for a ride. Lisa had a sigh of relief as they all walked calmly down the driveway.

But just as soon as they were out of sight, Lisa's heart began to pound. "Thump, thump," her heart went in her chest, so she ran into the house, got the keys to her van, and drove to catch up with the kids.

Now, following at a safe distance behind the four horses, her heart calmed as she watched over the children.

Chapter 14

Lindsay's Birthday

The Wrights had lived in their home in the country for just a little over a year, but this was Lindsay's first birthday celebration with a horse of her own, so it would be extra special.

Penny rode Bunny over every couple of days to see if Lindsay could ride with her. Lisa always went out on the trail with them because Lindsay wasn't yet allowed to ride without an adult. Sometimes after riding, Penny would put Bunny in the corral with Moon and Midnight while she went swimming with Lindsay, Jeffrey, and Beau.

Lisa liked Penny a lot and sometimes didn't know if she was her friend or Lindsay's friend; she just seemed to fit in somewhere in between. One lazy summer afternoon, Lisa had some questions for Penny. "So, Penny, your mom doesn't mind you out on the trail by yourself?"

"She used to ride with me all the time, but now she's too busy with my sister and brother and doesn't have a horse anymore, either. But she trusts Bun Bun. If I didn't have my Bunster, she wouldn't let me."

"Well, that's nice that you have a good horse and are allowed ride by yourself."

"Lindsay has a good horse, too," Penny said very maturely. "If you let Lindsay go out on the trail with me, I'd take good care of her and make sure nothing happened."

"You're right. Midnight is a good horse and I do trust Lindsay and Midnight completely. It's just that, well, what if, you know, a bad guy jumps out from behind an orange tree or something. Those are the kind of things that concern me."

Lindsay chimed in, "Mom, if any bad guys jump out from behind an orange tree, trust me, me and Midnight would charge them!"

Lisa laughed, "Penny, how old were you when your mom let you ride alone? I think I was about ten."

"Mom, I'm going to be ten in a week!" Lindsay blurted.

"Okay, maybe for your birthday you can go for a birthday ride," Lisa agreed.

"Cool!" Penny declared.

Lisa had birthday invitations in her hand and began writing Penny's name on the front of one, "Penny, what's your last name?"

"McKinney."

Lisa stopped writing and looked at Penny with a smile, "Did you say McKinney?"

"Uh huh"

"Your name is Penny McKinney?"

"Yep."

"Come on, you're kidding me," Lisa said. "Your last name is *not* McKinney."

"I am totally not kidding. That's my name, Penny McKinney," she said dramatically.

Lisa finished writing her last name on the invitation and handed it Penny, "Here you go

Penny McKinney. You are cordially invited to Lindsay's tenth birthday party."

Lisa couldn't get over the fact that Penny's last name rhymed with her first name and she said it again, "Penny McKinney, hmm, that's very cute. I once went to school with a Herby Derby."

Lindsay and Penny laughed and didn't believe Lisa. Lisa assured both girls that it was true.

On the morning of Lindsay's birthday, Lisa was up early making chocolate cupcakes, when Beau noticed and exclaimed, "Oh goody, pup cakes!"

Lindsay heard Beau's mistake from the hallway and corrected him, "Beau, don't you mean cupcakes?"

Lisa liked Beau's innocence and winked at Lindsay, "Beau's right, Lindsay. We're having pup cakes."

Lindsay stood by her mother and watched her swirl the chocolate batter around the bowl and just when she thought she could, she dove her finger into the batter and got a big finger-full and quickly put it in her mouth. However, the chocolate batter spilled across the counter, and down her pajamas and chin. "Lindsay, can't you wait until the *pup* cakes are done?" Lisa chided.

The next one in the kitchen that morning was Jeff. He picked up Lindsay and gave her a kiss on her cheek, "Happy birthday, Lindsay! I just can't believe you're ten years old today and you're getting prettier and prettier just like your mom!" Jeff winked at Lisa.

"Dad, now that I am ten, can I go on a trail ride all by myself? I mean with Penny. She's twelve and a half, Dad, and she has a really well-trained horse," Lindsay said convincingly.

"Why don't we go out for a birthday breakfast and talk about it," her father suggested.

What Lindsay didn't know was that her parents had already decided to let her go with Penny for a short trail ride. When Lindsay got back from her planned breakfast outing, there would be a surprise.

Right when Lindsay and her Dad left the driveway, Lisa went to work on her plan. She called

Penny and told her it was safe to come over. Then, with a bag full of balloons, ribbons and rubber bands, she walked up to the horse corrals. Today would be a day that Lindsay would never forget. Lisa bathed Midnight, making sure that his mane and tail were perfectly clean and shiny. Once Midnight was dry, she put Lindsay's favorite red crocheted ear bonnet on him, placing it perfectly over his ears and down his forehead. She blew up a small red balloon and attached it to his mane. One-by-one, she blew up different colored balloons and attached them all in a row down Midnight's neck. Next she French-braided just the top of his tail and attached three more balloons to it.

Midnight suddenly lifted his head high and gazed out over the property. Lisa looked in the same direction and saw Penny and Bunny cantering up the hill. Penny was riding with one hand and holding a birthday package with the other.

"Oh, my gosh!" Penny exclaimed. "Midnight looks so cool," she added, jumping down from Bunny. "Is Lindsay back yet?"

"She should be back any minute. Do you want to put Bunny in the corral?"

"No, that's okay; I'll just tie her up."

Lisa quickly saddled and bridled Midnight, making sure that everything was just right. "Do you want Bunny to have some balloons on her?"

"Yeah! Do you have any extra red ones?"

Lisa handed Penny a red balloon. Penny blew it up and just as she started to attach the balloon to Bunny's mane, she had second thoughts. "What if the balloon pops?"

"I didn't think about that," Lisa said, taking a second look at Midnight standing quietly covered with balloons.

"Bunny is good and all, but I highly doubt she will appreciate a balloon popping on her neck. On second thoughts, I think I'll pass on the balloons."

Right on time, Jeff and Lindsay arrived home. He drove Lindsay straight up to the horses, and before he could even fully stop his truck, Lindsay's door flew open. "Hi, Penny. Oh, Midnight, you look so cute," she said, hugging him. "Mom, Dad said I can ride with Penny."

Lindsay ran to the tack room and got her helmet and gloves. Lisa hoisted her 10-year-old daughter up on to her shiny black horse. Penny confidently climbed up into her western saddle. The girls were ready to go.

Penny walked over to Lindsay and handed her the present she carried over, "Happy birthday, Lindsay."

"Thank you, Penny!" Lindsay enthused.

"You can't open it right now. You have to wait until after we sing *Happy Birthday*, but you can shake it and guess what it is."

Lindsay pressed her ear to the present and shook. She shook and shook and shook the box, "I give up."

Lisa took the box from Lindsay and set it down. "You girls have to go riding now so you can be back for the party."

"Can I take Lindsay to my house?" Penny suggested.

"Where do you live?"

"I live just a little past Bill's. Down the canal, past the dip in the canal and across the open field

by the fig trees. My house is just across the field," assured Penny.

"Please, Mom, I really want to see where Penny lives," Lindsay begged.

"Okay, but please be careful."

"Oh, we will," the girls chorused.

As the girls set off together, Midnight snarled his nose and showed his teeth to Bunny. "Midnight!" Lindsay chided. The girls laughed and continued on down the hill and finally out of sight.

Lisa walked down the hill by herself, feeling proud. Proud that she had raised Lindsay up to be 10 years old. Proud that her daughter could be trusted on a horse, and happy that she had a friend. Back in the house, Lisa busied herself with getting things ready for the party, absolutely at ease that Lindsay was on her first trail ride without her.

Lindsay and Penny thoroughly enjoyed each others company. Lindsay admired Penny's pretty red saddle pad, and the red leg wraps on Bunny. "Penny," Lindsay started as they walked their horses down the canal, "what's your favorite color?"

"Red. It's obvious, huh? I just love for Bun Bun to wear red. I can't help it."

"Red is my favorite color, too."

"Then you are going to love your birthday present," Penny said.

"I will?"

"Yes, but that's the only thing I'm going to say about it. You're just going to have to wait to see what it is."

When the girls passed Murray's ranch, Midnight automatically wanted to turn in his driveway, but Lindsay pulled his reins and straightened him out. "Midnight, we're not going there today."

"Lindsay, when we get to my house, I want you to see my hedgehog."

Lindsay opened her eyes wide, "You have a hedgehog?"

"I'll let you hold it."

"Okay," Lindsay said skeptically.

Penny showed Lindsay the fig trees and each girl picked a fig as they passed by. "I love figs!" Penny said as she bit into the sweet delicate fruit.

Lindsay wasn't thrilled with figs but copied Penny's enthusiasm as she took a small bite of the fig she had picked.

"There's my house," Penny said pointing across the field.

"Your house is huge!" Lindsay exclaimed.

Penny's driveway and house looked too nice to take horses into but Penny didn't know any different. Penny got off Bunny and pressed a secret code to open the big iron entry gate.

"Are we allowed to walk our horses on your driveway?" Lindsay asked in concern.

"Yeah, don't even worry about it."

Lindsay got off Midnight and the girls walked their horses on the nice driveway toward Penny's big house. "I want my mom to see Midnight," Penny started and then yelled at the top of her lungs.

"Mom! Mom!"

Soon Penny's mom walked out of the house, "What on earth are you yelling for, Penny?"

"I want you to meet Lindsay and her horse, Midnight."

"Hi, Lindsay, I'm Penny's mom, Tina. Your horse is very pretty, and I like the balloons."

"Thank you."

"He must be a nice horse to be wearing balloons like that," said Penny's mom.

"Oh, he is!" Lindsay said dramatically. "One balloon popped on the way over here and he didn't even do anything," she said, pointing to a single popped balloon as evidence.

"Lindsay, you can just call her Mom, everyone else does," Penny said.

Penny looked just like her mom. They both had dark curly hair, fair skin and brown eyes.

"Come on, Lindsay, let's put the horses away and then you can see my hedgehog!" Penny led Bunny down to the lower part of their property and Lindsay followed with Midnight. Penny's house had a lot of fully grown trees that shaded their corrals. The girls took off their horse's bridles and saddles, and put each of them in their own corral. Penny threw both horses a flake of hay to snack on.

Once inside Penny's house, Penny introduced Lindsay to her little sister and her brother. Lindsay stuck close to Penny so she wouldn't get lost in her big house. Penny led Lindsay into her room and had her sit on her bed and cover her eyes while she got the hedgehog from its cage. "Okay, open them!"

Lindsay opened her eyes and, after seeing the strange critter, scooted back on the bed, "Actually, I don't think I want to hold it."

Penny laughed and said, "Don't worry, I promise it won't stick you."

Still, Lindsay hesitated. Then Penny had an idea, "I know, if I get my special gloves, then will you hold it?"

Lindsay scrunched her face. "Maybe."

Penny ran from her room and quickly came back with big, green, leather gloves and gave them to Lindsay. Lindsay put them on and when she realized that they covered her arms all the way up to her elbows, she held out her hands to accept the strange, prickly creature.

"What's its name?"

"Her name is Sonic"

Lindsay examined the spiky quills that covered the hedgehog and once she was satisfied, she

handed it back to Penny. Penny grabbed the tame critter and put it back in its cage. "Aren't you afraid of its quills?" Lindsay asked.

"Are you kidding? Sonic would never raise her quills at me," Penny answered confidently. "Let's go back to your house now, okay."

Meanwhile back at the Wright's, Lisa caught herself constantly looking out her living room window, scanning the property for a sign of the girls return. Her heart began to beat hard in her chest. Every minute that went by seemed like an hour. She walked back into the kitchen, and then right back out to the living room to check the property again. Able to stand waiting no longer, Lisa took action. She hurriedly went to the garage and pulled out her dusty bike with a flat tire. The previously proud, confident mother was now nervous and perspiring as she scanned the garage for a tire pump. Luckily, she soon found it and quickly pumped the tire back up to the right pressure and, just as she began to ride off, Jeff found her. "Where are you going?"

"I'm going to find Lindsay and Penny."

"Why? They're fine, don't worry about them," Jeff said confidently.

"Just watch the boys please, I'll be back soon," Lisa said as she pedaled her way out of the driveway. She pedaled and pedaled her way down their long driveway, going as fast as she could.

Fast and furiously, she headed down the canal and tried to remember where Penny said she lived. As Lisa approached Bill Murray's ranch, she thought a short cut through the orange groves would save time. Bumpety, bump over the uneven soil she went, pedaling harder and faster, the orange tree branches flipped and flapped and slapped her in the face.

She didn't care; she was on a mission to find her 10-year-old daughter.

On their way back to Lindsay's house, Penny picked yet another fig but Lindsay didn't. Once the girls reached the canal, Penny looked at Lindsay and asked, "Do you want to race to Bill's field?"

"Sure," Lindsay said as she gathered her reins.

Without even one more word, the girls were off galloping along the canal. Midnight grunted

and blew his nose and all at once surged forward and passed Bunny.

The pretty yellow Quarter Horse was fast, but Midnight was faster. The girls laughed and when they got to Bill's field, the dirt flew up in a cloud as they slowed their horses down to a walk. "Wow, I didn't know your horse could run that fast," Penny exclaimed.

Lindsay bent down over Midnight's neck and laughed, "Did you hear him grunt?"

Penny laughed, "How could I miss it? How old is he again?"

"He's twenty."

Penny leaned forward and talked directly to her horse, "Bunny, did you hear that? You let a twenty-year-old gelding beat you!"

"Midnight loves to run," Lindsay said. "It's the Thoroughbred in him."

"Well, Bunny loves to run, too, but now after seeing Midnight run, I'm not so sure." Penny said and then went on complaining, "That is *so* not fair, a twenty-year-old beat us!"

As the girls went on chatting, Bunny and Midnight perked up their ears listening to something in the orange groves. "What do you hear, Bun Bun?" Penny asked her horse. Then, both horses flinched as Lindsay's mother suddenly popped out of the grove on her bike.

"Mom!" Lindsay exclaimed, "what are you doing? You scared us!"

Lisa was just as surprised to see the girls as they were to see her. "Hi, girls, how's your ride going?" Lisa asked, out of breath.

Lindsay chuckled, "Our ride is going fine, but you have red marks on your face and a branch in your hair!"

Lisa rubbed her face, and nonchalantly pulled the branch out of her hair as if she was never nervous.

"We were just on our way home, Mom." explained Lindsay.

"Oh, then I guess I'll follow you the rest of the way home."

As Lisa pedaled her bike behind the horses, Lindsay and Penny told her every detail about the race between Bunny and Midnight.

Friends and family filled the Wright house for Lindsay's birthday celebration. Lindsay swam with Penny, Jeffrey, and Beau and they all laughed as they talked about how funny Beau looked when Mighty Mouse took off with him down the driveway. Even Sugar swam in the pool that hot day. Lindsay saved Penny's present for last and when she opened it, her heart leapt; it was a brand new red halter and lead rope for Midnight.

That night, when Lindsay thought her celebration had come to an end and she crawled into bed, her mother said she had one last surprise. Before Lisa would tell her, she tucked Lindsay's blankets tightly all around her and pushed her hair back from her face getting her full attention.

"Lindsay, you love Midnight right?"

"Yeah," she said, happy they were on the subject of Midnight.

"Okay, well, what I want to tell you is that you and Midnight will be spending a lot more time together."

"What do you mean?"

"Dad and I have signed you up for Pony Club."

With a smile she asked, "What's Pony Club?"

"Pony Club is an organization that teaches kids all about horses. You'll ride with kids your own age and study with them as well."

"I will?"

"Yes, you will and the best part of all is that it's held on Grace St. just down from Anne's house, so you can ride there yourself."

"When do I start?"

"You'll start in the fall. But for now you need to get some sleep, you've had a big day. Goodnight, I love you."

Lindsay closed her eyes, but couldn't get the smile off her face.

It truly had been an unforgettable birthday.

The Windsor Heights Series

Windsor Heights

To The Country

Moon and Midnight

The Auction

The Great Gift

Sugar and Cheyenne

Dazzle

The Black Gelding

Windsor Heights Coloring Book, Volume I

Windsor Heights Coloring Book, Volume II